Race
to
Velasco

Paul N. Spellman

Race to Velasco

by Paul N. Spellman

 Hendrick-Long Publishing Co.
P.O. Box 25123 • Dallas, Texas
75225

Library of Congress Cataloging-in-Publication Data

Spellman, Paul N.
    Race to Velasco / by Paul N. Spellman.
        p.   cm.
    Summary: Henry Woods and Antonio Gonzales head for
adventure with rebel Texans at the Battle of Velasco before the
Texas Revolution.
    ISBN 1-885777-01-9 (alk. paper)
    [1. Frontier and pioneer life—Texas. 2. Adventure and
adventurers—Fiction. 3. Texas—History—To 1846.] I. Title.
PZ 7.S74725Rac   1995
[Fic]—dc20   95-606
                                                                CIP
                                                                AC

10 9 8 7 6 5 4 3 2 1

Cover design by Dianne J. Borneman,
Shadow Canyon Graphics, Evergreen, Colorado.

The text paper used in this book exceeds the minimum require-
ments of the American National Standard (ANSI) for permanence
of paper and printed library materials. (Acid Free Permanence)

Hendrick-Long Publishing Co.

Dallas, Texas 75225

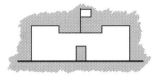

Historical Introduction

The Law of April 6, 1830, changed the lives of the Americans who had colonized the Mexican province known as Coahuila-Texas. Before the new laws, settlers had been encouraged to immigrate into the northern Mexico regions. The borders remained open and busy, allowing hundreds of families, some with slaves, to move to the settlements of the empresarios. In addition to the cities of San Antonio de Bexar and Nacogdoches, the communities of Gonzales, San Felipe, Goliad, and Indianola grew quickly.

Concerned by some of the independent thinking of these many American colonists, the Mexican government placed restrictions designed to discourage others from coming across the Sabine and Red River borders.

Slaves could no longer be bought, sold, or brought into Texas. The Mexican army marched into the northern province to enforce border restrictions and collect duties (import taxes) along the Gulf Coast. Law and order remained in the hands of local commandants under orders to "keep the peace." American colonists could not request jury trials nor expect any sympathy when they complained about jail sentences or fines.

This change in the laws caused many colonists to become bitter and angry toward their government. The complaining increased. Mexican soldiers and customs officials tightened security. Angry outbursts in Anahuac and Velasco, port areas, resulted in mob scenes, violence, and arrests.

Both sides of the disputes grew increasingly nervous as the situation worsened.

The Battle at Velasco Fort in June of 1832 brought these fears and feelings to the surface. An angry, armed mob of Texan colonists set out to release three of their friends unjustly jailed at Anahuac. Others headed for the round stockade on the Velasco beach to shut down the customs office and force the Mexican soldiers there out of the area.

As a result of this all-night battle on June 26th, the fort temporarily fell into the hands of a Texan force. The Mexican government at Anahuac had agreed to release the colonists in jail and relieve the duties officer of his job. For their part, the colonists agreed to return to their homes peacefully, accept the basic points of the new law, and not allow the situation to get out of hand.

But the situation had changed forever. For the next three years, negotiations, demands, and more Mexican soldiers in Texas brought the entire region closer to outright war. If not for a deadly outbreak of cholera across Mexico in 1833 and 1834, which kept both the Mexican government and the Texas colonists isolated in their communities, the Texas revolution may very well have been remembered as starting that night on the beach at Velasco.

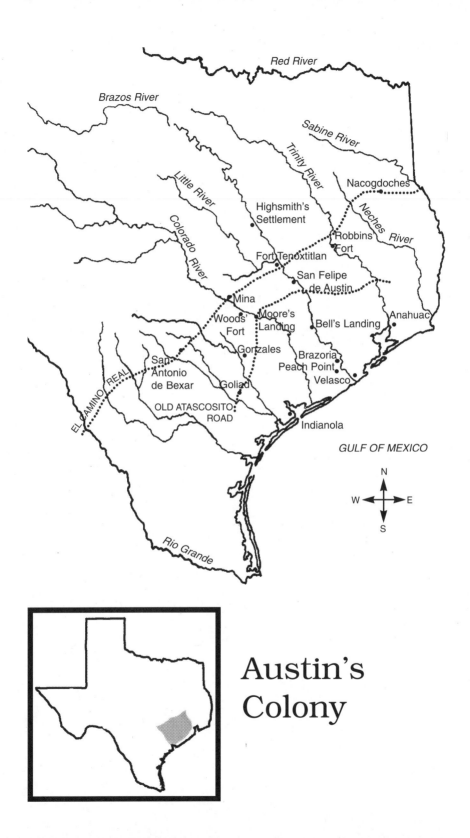

Austin's
Colony

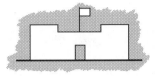

Chapter One

Faster! Run faster! He heard the voice inside pleading with him to hurry. His legs pumped harder and the ground in front of him seemed to jump toward him at every step. He felt the sweat running down his temples. His buckskin shirt was soaked with perspiration. He wasn't sure he could keep up this pace, but the voice of desperation hadn't given up on him yet. He willed his knees to bend harder and faster, his arms to reach through the dry air ahead of him as if he were swimming instead of running for his life.

Up ahead, a stand of trees beckoned him to come and hide behind them. He remembered that the river swelled and ran just on the other side of the trees. If only he could make it as far as the river! If he could slide beneath the protective surface of the water, he would be safe. He could float away from his enemy and swim to the safety of his village, where his father waited. The thought of being rescued added energy to his short but strong legs, and he felt his speed increase a fraction more. He would make it! He had to get to the trees!

The screams! He heard them again, or maybe just sensed them from somewhere deep inside his heart. The terrifying voices surrounded him like the blackening storms that would suddenly come upon his village in the spring. Darkness and terror, children crying and mothers holding them tightly as the thunder echoed like great drums across the prairie. He remembered now, as his heart thumped to the same beat as his racing feet.

There had been three of them. They had been just as startled as he, nearly walking into one another as they crossed paths in the deep prairie grass. He had been away from the village all that morning, leaving quietly before first light and traveling quickly with his face toward the rising sun. In his fright now, he forgot why he had started out that morning. Had he been hunting? Or was he just exploring, practicing the many skills his father had taught him? It didn't matter now! He was being hunted, and there was no one to help him. Only the skills could save him!

He knew that if he looked over his shoulder, it would slow his speed. But he had to see if they had kept up the pace, or had he outdistanced them? He managed a quick glance behind him.

He saw them, and their shouts frightened him as noise pounded in his ears. Their swift, smooth steps looked much longer than his. The one closest to him now had a terrible grin on his face, and his right arm pumped the air, a wave in his direction that was unfriendly as the clenched fist that bore down on him. Behind him, the other two kept the pace as well. He saw the war feathers brandished in their hair. Each warrior had two white feathers, blown straight back from the gray headbands as they ran after him.

The trees seemed almost in reach now. How many more steps? Thirty? He guessed to himself, measuring the distance against the enemy's position behind him. They had gained only a step in the minutes since they had begun the chase. He gulped the air as if it would add more energy to each step.

Twenty paces now, no more than that, he felt sure. If he had been listening, he might have been able to hear the swift waters up ahead, waiting to rescue him. For now, his keen sense of hearing would do him no good. Only his legs mattered—and his eyes. He kept one eye on the ground just ahead of each step, watching for limbs or rabbit holes that would trip him, forcing the grassy plains to pass under his feet, reaching for the motte of slender trunks and the river bank just beyond.

Ten more steps. Five. He raced into the cover of the trees and turned to his right, onto a path that ran alongside the river, a path he knew well, a friend. For a brief moment, he knew that his enemies had lost sight of him. It gained him two steps, as they slowed to look which way he had gone. But they picked up speed quickly in his direction, the third warrior cutting across the intersecting paths and taking the lead now.

Where was the best place to breach the water's surface? His mind raced along with his body, measuring the moment when he must leave the reassuring ground beneath his feet and launch himself through the air and into the river. A terrifying shout pierced the air just behind him, answering his question for him.

His feet left the ground as his knees bent and propelled him into the air. He seemed to float in slow motion for an instant, his arms stretched out in front of him, his legs straightened to form a long, smooth line diving for the surface. He held his breath, as if it would help the motion of the dive.

His fingertips brushed the water's surface just as the arrow thumped into his thigh. He remembered his face being splashed by the river, and the first strike of pain from just above his right knee. Then, nothing more.

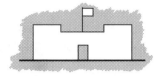

Chapter Two

In his dream, the great white beast came out of the billowy clouds far above his village. He heard no sound in his dream, and saw only "tatanka" bearing down on the children who played with the dogs near the creek. They weren't watching, weren't paying attention. No one else seemed to notice the great and terrible hooves that bore down on the village from above. Only he, Crooked Path, saw the bison. He must rescue the village. His father would be proud, and would sit with the other warriors to tell the story of his son, the young brave who had saved all of the families that day.

Crooked Path stood at the edge of the village, a gleaming knife in his right hand, awaiting the monster. Closer and closer it came, dropping from the skies and now onto the prairie. Its terrible breath condensed in front of his red eyes as he stormed toward the young warrior. Unafraid, Crooked Path stood his ground and waited.

The white beast closed the distance to Crooked Path and lowered its great shaggy head as it charged. A shaft of sunlight burst upon the gleaming horns on its head, and the brave's knife sliced through the air. An awful sound, a low bellowing growl, broke the soundlessness of the dream, and grisly ivory teeth buried themselves into his leg.

Crooked Path awoke to the sound of his own scream of pain, and the shooting stabs that coursed up his leg. He lay on a soft mat of grass in the shade of an old, gnarled oak tree. He lay on his back, his right leg propped up on a severed limb that had fallen from the tree. Sweat glistened across his neck and chest, and his breathing was labored. He glanced down to the source of the terrible pain. A tourniquet was wrapped around his thigh, just inches above his knee. Dried blood, brown and crusting, covered both of his legs, and even spotted his stomach.

He looked to his left and saw the broken arrow that had once imbedded itself in his leg. Now it lay broken and helpless beside him. He wanted to grab it and throw it as far away as he could, but his arms failed him at that moment, and his left hand flopped onto the ground like a fish on the river bank.

Crooked Path looked between his feet, and saw a shape swaying in the shadows by the tree.

His enemy, standing in the shadows, waited to kill him! Crooked Path must get away! He lifted his head and shoulders off the ground, searching for a message to tell his legs to move. Instead, he fell back to the grassy pillow. In his dizzy mind, he remembered only that the shape moved closer to him and bent down beside him. Then, he passed out again.

"Hey, you," a voice somewhere whispered. "Hey. Wake up. Are you all right?"

Crooked Path opened his eyes slowly. A face stared down into his, only inches away. Two blue eyes gaped at him. A smile creased this stranger's face, but it certainly wasn't the enemy who had been chasing him. In fact, this face looked small, like his own, only lighter in color.

"Are you waking up?" the voice asked. "Can you talk?" The stranger stood up now, away from Crooked Path until the face connected now with shoulders and arms and legs. The stranger brushed back a tuft of blond hair from his forehead and smiled again. "You all right?"

"My leg," Crooked Path began, "my leg hurts."

"I 'spect so," the stranger replied. "Had an arrow in it."

"Where am I?" Crooked Path suddenly remembered what had happened before he passed out. He had been running, chased by three of his enemy. The trees. The river. The arrow piercing his leg. Where were they? Was he still in danger? Who was this strange boy, who seemed friendly and looked about his own age? The stranger's voice interrupted the questions.

"—out of the river. You'd kinda washed up on the bank when I spotted you. I pulled you out and laid you down here. That's when I noticed the arrow. You were out, so I broke the shaft and cut out the arrowhead, bandaged you up."

"The ones who chased me, who shot me?"

"Don't know. Didn't see anyone around. Just you, laying there."

Crooked Path lay back on the ground and thought about the situation. Was he safe after all?

"You're gonna need some help with that leg. I did what I could, out here, but we need to get you cleaned up good, or you'll lose that leg." The stranger looked around, as if planning his next move. A horse whinnied from the other side of the big tree. "I think I can get you to my house all right. My horse'll carry us fine."

"I need to get to my village. My father will care for me." Crooked Path struggled once more to sit up, and fell back again.

"Don't know 'bout that," the boy said. "Better not be ridin' into an Indian village without my being announced." He emphasized the last word for effect. "Lemme get you to my house."

Crooked Path saw little possibility of arguing. He could not move on his own, and who knew how far he had come down the river, how far now to his own village. He looked up at the stranger.

Perhaps this was a friend. He stretched his hand up from the ground. The stranger bent over and began to hoist him carefully to his feet, making sure the weight on his injured leg transferred to his own shoulders.

They limped gingerly toward the horse tethered at the tree.

"By the way," said the stranger, "my name's Henry Woods."

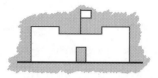

Chapter Three

Henry sat down on the dirt floor next to the cot where Crooked Path slept. The Indian boy had dozed off several times since they'd ridden into Woods' Fort earlier that day. It had been a pretty rough ride down the Colorado. The Indian's leg had started bleeding again, and by the time they'd reached home, blood caked Henry's saddle and his horse's hide. Henry's mother, Minerva, had dressed the wound and cleaned Crooked Path's leg. Now the boy slept fitfully, occasionally crying out in his own language, then drifting back to his bad dreams.

"Comanche arrow," the old man muttered. His long, white hair was disheveled and fell down in his face as he stood over the Indian boy. "They're the worst, Henry. You remember that."

"Yessir," Henry replied quickly, "but what about this one?"

"Tonkawa. Look at his breechcloth. See the animal bones and teeth hanging down on those leather thongs? Tonkawa do that. Tells everyone they're hunters, protects them from bad spirits, too."

Henry glanced at the sleeping Indian. "Are the Tonkawa dangerous, Pa?"

Zadock Woods thought about his answer for a moment. "Never can tell for sure. Usually not. They hate the Comanche—blood enemies go way back before time, I reckon. Good scouts when we've needed them on the frontier. Good hunters. Fish, too, and seen some of them planting crops up on the other side of the Brazos."

"They ever hunt Texans, Pa?"

"I heard some stories once. 'Bout some trouble on the Little River, north of here. Two of Colonel Austin's rangers got into a shoot-out with some Tonkawas, both sides shot up pretty good. Could be the rangers were a little out of their area, walked into trouble." He looked at the sleeping boy. "This one's not much trouble, I'd say."

After supper, Henry and his brother, Leander, had talked into the night about the Indians. Leander knew plenty of stories, some that Pa had told about the Missouri days, when the Sauk and the Fox had stirred up trouble over in Illinois. Henry's favorite stories were about Black Hawk, the chief who had led a confederacy of tribes against the white men twenty years before.

Henry's father had fought in those wars, protecting the families who had moved to Missouri Territory. The Woods family had come all the way from Vermont and Massachusetts to live on the frontier, along with others from New York and Kentucky, Virginia and Pennsylvania.

As Leander talked into the darkness, Henry drifted off to sleep, dreaming of Black Hawk and Comanches and broken arrows.

First light glinted through the fort's portal and directly into Henry's face. He squinted, partly asleep, and heard the rustling of buckskin against the cot across the room. Henry sat up and watched as the Indian boy attempted to get to his feet. He lost his balance three times before he managed to take a step toward the door. The injured boy looked around carefully, then reached for the door.

"Wait," Henry whispered loud enough for the boy to hear him without waking the others, "you can't leave yet." Henry got up and walked to the Indian. "You're hurt too bad."

"I need to go," said Crooked Path, "my father will come looking for me soon. I must go home."

"Hold on. I'll saddle up my horse, and take you."

"No. You cannot come to my village. I will go there alone."

But Henry would not budge from the doorway until the Indian agreed to some help. Mounting the old bay once more, the two boys headed up the Colorado at a steady gait, watching the shadows flee the light of the dawn at their back.

They rode for two hours, until Crooked Path motioned for Henry to stop. Dismounting, the Indian boy looked up at Henry.

"Thank you for helping. I am Crooked Path, son of Eagle-That-Soars, a great warrior. If we meet again, it will be in peace." Crooked Path raised his right arm in Henry's direction, then turned and disappeared into the tall prairie grass.

Henry rode back along the same trail, spotting the tree where he had carried the wounded Indian from the riverbank. He glanced out across the river, and wondered if the Comanches were still around, the ones who had shot Crooked Path. A shudder ran down his spine, and Henry urged his horse a little faster along the trail. He was not afraid, exactly, but this sure seemed a good place to be caught by a Comanche. Not much place to hide, a pretty good race back to the fort, no other communities or farms around except . . .

Antonio! Of course! His friend Antonio lived just south of here, across the rise and down the creek that twisted through the small hills. Won't Antonio be surprised to hear what happened! He'll want to hear all about it, that was for sure.

Henry turned the bay's head south, and picked up the gait until they rode a good pace to reach the Gonzales place before noon. Over the last rise, Henry spotted the small ranch that belonged to Señor Gonzales. The house stood in the front, and behind it lay the cook shanty that hid a small corral and barn. A dozen or so of the cattle that Antonio's father raised wandered over by a water tank.

Two hundred yards from the corral, Henry saw Antonio coming around from behind the barn. Henry let out his best war whoop and dug his heels into the bay's haunches, causing the old workhorse to snort, toss its head, and pick up speed, but not without a slight buck of irritation. Antonio turned at the sound, and made a dash to the front of the corral, waving his big sombrero back at his friend. As the gap closed between them, Henry started into his tale almost before the Mexican boy could understand what he was saying.

"Tonio, you'll never guess what happened!" Henry yelled. "I saved an Indian on the river yesterday! He was shot and drowning, and I pulled him out of the river and bandaged him up and took him home and . . ."

"Slow down, compadre," Antonio laughed and pointed at Henry, "you're talking too fast. Get down and start over again."

Henry slowed the old bay until he could handle the leap to the ground, and, in a second bounce, he straddled the corral fence next to Antonio, who waited patiently for the rider to catch his breath. For the next several minutes, Henry related the incidents that had led to his discovery of the Indian boy. "He's Tonkawa, Pa told me, named Crooked Path," he said, before describing the Comanche arrow that had been imbedded in the Indian's leg.

"My father has told us of the Comanches in the area," responded Antonio at that point. "There are scouting parties wandering from here to Mina, and even over to Moore's Landing."

"Moore's Landing? That's east of the fort," Henry said with surprise. "Comanches don't come there much. Way off their path."

"Father says we must be careful when we leave the ranchero. We are not to leave alone, and we must let him or Mother know." Antonio stared off into space, as if conjuring up an image of the Comanches hunting down the Tonkawa boy, arrows flying through the Texas air.

"Tonio, come with me. Let me show you where I found the Tonkawa. We'll look for tracks, see if we can find where the Comanches were headed."

"Mother has just called for us to eat," Antonio replied. "Come eat with us. Then we'll go."

Henry and his friend walked over to the house, where Maria Gonzales greeted them with hugs and plates filled with tamales and beans and tortillas. Both boys ate silently, sneaking a look at each other as if sharing a great secret.

After the meal, the boys said goodbye to Antonio's mother. Henry remembered to thank her for the fine vittles, and then the two friends headed for the open prairie along the Colorado. It would be a fine adventure today!

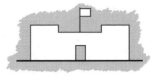

Chapter Four

The flashing yellow split in the dark sky, tinged with a green border, hinted at an even more dangerous weapon of nature now forming in the swirling black clouds above. The brilliant light suddenly cast on the boys and their horse caused all three to stare up into the sky. The accompanying sound of the thunderbolt's power echoed like an explosion, enveloping the two teen-agers and nearly picking them off the ground.

Henry's horse reared its head in fright and, at the same moment, managed to step right into a crevice dug alongside the trail he had been wandering. His front right leg buckled and he stumbled to regain his balance. Henry pulled tightly on the reins, bringing his mount under control and to a stop.

As the raindrops began pelting the boys like small pebbles thrown from across the old sand quarry back at the fort, Henry bent down to survey the damage on his old friend's foreleg.

"I don't feel any break," Henry finally shouted to Antonio through the noise of the gathering storm. "He pulled a muscle, I reckon."

"Will he be all right?" Antonio asked. He glanced around him just briefly, wondering about being so far from any of the places he knew.

"I reckon so," Henry shook his head and added, "but we're not going anywhere on his back for awhile."

Henry grabbed the reins and rubbed the horse's leg several times. The bay didn't jump, but he would be favoring that leg for the next few days. Henry pulled the horse's head close to his own, whispering a comforting word to his traveling companion while rubbing the top of his head.

Henry turned to Antonio. "You look like a cat just thrown in a well," he laughed. Water dripped steadily from Antonio's sombrero down past his shoulders; his boots mired in the rising mud.

"You don't look any better, mi amigo." True enough. Henry's tousled hair matted with the now-pouring rain, every inch of him sopping wet.

"We'd better look for shelter somewhere," Henry finally acknowledged. "This rain won't be stopping any time soon."

Taking the reins, Henry gingerly led the old bay back onto the trail, or what was left of it now that the rain had covered the prairie, and headed away from the strengthening windstorm. Henry found it impossible now to see more than a few yards ahead. The rain came down in blinding sheets, and only the occasional strike of lightning lit up the trail they tried to follow.

After about ten minutes heading generally eastward, Antonio shouted and pointed toward what looked like a grove of trees up ahead. As Henry nodded his head and pointed in agreement, the bay snorted twice and seemed to look back over its shoulder. At that instant the two boys heard the sound.

Tornado! There was no other sound like it that either had ever heard before. Once, two years earlier, a twister had touched down not far from Woods' Fort, tearing huge trees out of the ground and flinging them five hundred yards in every direction. Henry had never forgotten the sound that afternoon, and now the memory leaped back to mind for a brief instant.

Antonio broke into a dead run, heading for the trees and shelter. Henry tried to shout at him to stop. There was no time. Tonio would never reach the grove in time. Henry let the horse's reins go, and the old bay staggered off on its own. Henry could only hope his riding pal would be safe. Henry dove into a shallow recession five steps off the trail, and covered his head with both arms. Face down in the mud, the fourteen-year-old held his breath as the terrible wind-storm descended onto the prairie, less than a quarter-mile from where he lay.

Antonio kept running, his sombrero now in his left hand, helping pump his body along faster. The tornado bore down on him like a wrathful enemy looking only to destroy. The wind uprooted prairie grass and small prickly pear and flung debris into the ebony sky. Mud and water spewed in every direction, painting the land in shades of brown and gray.

Antonio slid and then somersaulted the last steps into the shelter of the elm motte. He rolled out of control, coming to an abrupt halt as his side struck a tree. A groan spilled from his lungs as the breath was knocked out of him, and he lay panting for a moment until he could inhale once more. Mud and bits of debris settled in his mouth and covered his face. Antonio did not remember spitting the mud in that instant, only the horrible sound of something being wrenched from its foundation against its will.

The tree Antonio had grabbed seemed to rise into the air, and the thirteen-year-old could only hold tighter to the flying object that had once been a sheltering elm. Antonio saw the ground falling away below him, fifteen feet, then thirty and forty. The tree turned him upside down for a moment, then twirled round and round. His legs splayed out from his body and from the tree where his arms remained firmly wound.

It seemed that everything moved in slow motion now. Antonio thought he could see other trees in the air beside him, catapulted from the earth and now dancing a grotesque step in mid-air. Did he see a jackrabbit literally fly by in front of him? And the noise! It shattered his eardrums, and he heard himself screaming sounds and words he did not understand.

Then, as suddenly as the tornado had come to the prairie and lifted Antonio into the sky, it disappeared, angrily sucking up into the deep clouds from where it had come. It was as if something, or someone, had called the twister back home, and it had responded in grudging obedience, kicking everything around it one last time.

Antonio remained still, his arms wrapped around the elm tree. But the motion had ceased, the noise gone. Only a lightly falling rain beat a smoother, calmer rhythm on his back now. He lay where he had been deposited for a full minute before cautiously looking around.

Nothing looked familiar. The tree rested at a crazy angle, its roots gently rocking in the light breeze, like a spiderweb that had been strewn across a barn wall. Other trees, or parts of trees, lay around him. One large limb had been tossed only inches from his head, and a pile of dismembered sticks settled off to his right.

How far had he flown through the air, he wondered? A mile? Or more? And in what direction? And Henry! Where was his friend? The frightening thought of injury to his companion brought Antonio up quickly to his feet. He scraped mud from his pants legs and tried to shake huge gray globs from his boots as he peered in every direction.

To get a better view of his surroundings, Antonio climbed carefully up onto the fallen tree that had been his flying machine a few minutes earlier. Getting his bearings, he finally decided that he had not traveled more than two hundred yards from where the trail now filled with muddy pools.

Two things sprang to mind at the same time: he had survived the "flight" miraculously uninjured; but, he now stood across the tributary from where he had first grabbed the tree! Ten paces from where the tree had landed, the swollen creek now coursed out of its banks, carrying tree limbs and tumbleweeds crazily along an uninvited path. He, Antonio, was fine. He told himself he must remember to say a prayer of thanksgiving. If Henry had survived the storm, he was now probably on the other side of a now impassable creekbed.

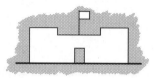

Chapter Five

Henry lay prostrate in the narrow ditch that had been his hiding place from the twister. Mud caked around his ears, and a sloshing sound came whenever he tried to move an arm or leg. Stuck!

He could lift his head out of the muck, which, he realized, had kept him from drowning face down in the depression. A huge amount of mud and sticks across his back and legs weighed him down. Every attempt to lift himself free only succeeded in sinking him an inch deeper. The ground had turned into quicksand.

The rain continued to come down, but the sky began to clear: he could at least see that out of the corner of one eye. The wind had died. An eerie stillness spread on to the soggy prairie. He heard no birds, no crickets, only the soft patter of raindrops around his head. Henry lay very still, and tried to recall what his father might have taught him that would help this predicament.

"Look about you, son," he could almost hear his father's deep, quiet voice, "survey your situation." His father had been a surveyor in Missouri, he recalled, before they had moved to Texas. What a fine time to be remembering that!

He looked around, turning his head carefully, not wanting to encourage his shoulders to sink any deeper into the gray mud. The prairie grass lay flattened against the ground in all directions. The trees seemed very far away. Nothing in reach to pull himself out. A mighty poor situation, he concluded quickly.

Perhaps if he tried to move just one hand, or even a few fingers at a time, he could control the sinking. Mentally, he chose his right hand, his brain sending a signal through the muscles of his shoulder and down his right arm. A finger wiggled, then two. So far, so good. His thumb came free, and then his wrist. The elbow sprung loose with a squishing sound, and Henry twisted his shoulders just enough to regain some balance against the quicksand.

Now the second arm. It came free with a little more effort, but now his shoulders and both arms moved. Henry lifted himself up onto his elbows. The mud gave way a few inches, but he froze his movement, and the sinking stopped. He turned his attention down past his waist. Glancing over his left shoulder, he saw both of his legs completely buried under the gray surface.

Several pulls from the elbows resulted only in another inch lost to the earth. Ahead of him, he saw no trunk, no root, no rock that he might reach.

Facing east, away from where the tornado had come spilling from the sky, he could still tell that dusk had come and the sun had likely set behind the thick cloud cover. Darkness settled around him now, and his predicament loomed all the more dangerous with nightfall. Animals would be roaming this battered prairie for victims of the storm. Coyotes or wolves would soon howl their warning invitations to the night's adventures.

Henry didn't think he wanted to be a coyote's midnight snack, but he couldn't figure a solution to his problem. That thought passed just as he heard the noise.

The rustling sound, muted by the mud and rainfall, seemed very close, and directly behind him. Henry measured the footsteps of the beast, and thought it might be some five paces to his back. Be still, he commanded himself. Pretend to be dead, perhaps the beast will wander by.

But the steps closed in on him now, practically on top of his buried legs. Henry could almost sense the musty breath of the animal now upon him, and the first hint of fear coursed through his nerves. His shoulders twitched. He figured he could make one sudden twist from his elbows, and deliver a fist into the face of the attacker. Henry took a breath, measured the distance in his head, and twisted. His fist shot through the air, mud flying off his wrist. The knuckles of his balled right hand smacked their target just above the nose.

His old bay! The horse snorted and reared its head in surprise that his rider would strike him for no reason. He shook his head, the mane splattering water in all directions, the reins spilling down onto the wet earth just where Henry's waist should be.

The reins! Henry coaxed his old friend around to face him. He grabbed the reins and hollered for the horse to step back, step back, and again, another step. The bay stumbled. Henry remembered the injury and spoke softly that things would be just fine.

The horse's weight countered the quicksand, and slowly but surely Henry found himself freed from his muddy grave. The earth seemed to object at first, holding on to his legs and feet with great determination. His left boot nearly came off, but Henry grabbed it by the top as it appeared at the surface.

Finally free! He stood up and looked down at the ditch where he had hidden from the storm. The mud re-formed itself almost immediately and, with one last gurgling sound, settled as if nothing, or no one, had ever been trapped there. Henry turned and walked away, brushing the sticky substance from his face and neck.

Where to now, old pal? Henry thought, directing the question to anyone who might be reading his mind. He looked around him. The devastation startled him. Nothing had escaped the destructive force of the twister.

Tonio! Where was he? Henry remembered the dash for the grove of trees, then the awful sound of the tornado, and diving into the soupy ditch. Had the storm taken his friend away? He started to run, stumbling along as the darkness gathered around him, headed for the trees where he had seen Tonio running.

When he reached the place where he thought his friend had gone, he realized that something was very wrong! Of course, even in the dim light still teasing the prairie, Henry could tell that the trees had disappeared, slung into the skies by the killer-wind. Had that same storm taken Antonio with it?

"HENRY!" The familiar voice screamed his name from the darkness off to his right. Tonio had survived! But where exactly was he now?

"TONIO!" Henry cried the name in the direction of the voice he had heard.

"Henry, this way, I'm over here!"

"Hang on, Tonio, I'm coming!" Henry let go of the horse's reins, confident the bay would not get lost again, and took off running for his friend. He heard the sound of the rushing stream at the same instant that his left foot stepped onto the slippery bank. He tried desperately to stop himself. Too late!

Henry managed a very poor cartwheel, falling into the roily river. His shout spilled into the darkness as he splashed below the surface. The water enveloped him and pulled him away to the middle of the current's path. He struggled to the surface once, then fell below, and again a second time. He grabbed out in all directions, and his right hand fell on a limb of sufficient girth to hold his head above the waters.

"HENRY!" He heard Tonio's voice, very close to where he floated along. But not in control of his journey at the moment, he could only cry out some garbled word that had tried to be "Help!"

In the next moment, Henry heard a large splash from the general direction of Tonio's voice. Breathing hard, Henry clambered up until all but his legs lay across the tree trunk, and he held on for dear life to his makeshift raft. A hand appeared in front of his face! Tonio! He had dived into the water to rescue Henry, and now the two of them both needed rescuing!

"Henry," Tonio panted, "you all right?"

"Sure," Henry answered between struggling breaths, "you come here to save me or something?" He managed a wry smile.

The two boys stared through the darkness at each other. Henry laughed first. Antonio followed with a "Whoop!" The two pals grabbed hands and hung on together. Somewhere, down this roving stream, things would surely turn out all right.

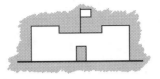

Chapter Six

Henry Woods' family listened with rapt attention as the two young adventurers related each moment of their day and night on the prairie and down the raging stream.

The floating tree had eventually lodged against a pile of debris already cast down the creekbed, and the boys had climbed off their "raft" and onto the safety of the muddy bank. They traveled less than a half-mile, and soon, with the bay mount recovered as well, hiked their way through the pitch darkness toward home. Sometime before dawn, they had lay down for a quick nap, choosing the high ground of a hillock at the edge of the prairie to make camp.

After a stopover at Antonio's house to reassure his parents, the two had continued on to the fort. Henry put up the bay in the stable after rubbing him down and feeding him. Minerva Woods cooked up a hearty breakfast of beans and grits and bacon, and the two teens devoured it all, washing the meal down with a pitcher of goat's milk.

Now, story time came to an end. The midday chores needed finishing, at least for Zadock and Leander. But the boys insisted on accompanying the men while Minerva cleared the table and began preparations for the evening supper.

A fence post out behind the fort had been pushed out of its position by a roving steer sometime that morning. Zadock and Leander set about the task of replacing it. Henry's father, even at age fifty-five, amazed the boys with his tireless energy and strength. With the two younger ones pitching in by dragging the split post away and to its new position, the job went quickly.

As sweat soaked their clothes, they stopped to drink from a pail of well water. The casual conversation soon turned to the politics of the day.

"Josiah Wilbarger came by the other day, Leander," Zadock spoke up, "while you were tending Montraville's cattle. He allowed that the situation on the coast is getting worse every day."

"What's to be done, Pa?" Leander asked. He loved talking about the news of happenings around Texas, and of the growing trouble near Velasco and Anahuac, two ports on the Gulf of Mexico. "What does Mr. Austin say?"

Henry and Antonio's interest perked up when they heard the name. Austin. Mr. Stephen Austin was the leader of the colony where they lived, where most of the Texans were coming to live. He spoke for most of the people, talking to the Mexican governor in San Antonio whenever problems arose. He was a man to be respected.

". . . the tax collector's there." Henry's father had just finished his response.

"Can we do anything?" Leander's voice rose in anticipation. Here loomed an opportunity to defend the rights of the Texans against the Mexican government that seemed intent in taking those rights away.

For two years, the Mexican governor had been increasing restrictions across Austin's Colony, and all the way up to the Sabine River and Nacogdoches. Mexico allowed fewer Americans to come into Texas, and none could bring slaves with them. On the coast, men had come and set up offices to collect taxes—duties they called them—from all of the ships moving to and from New Orleans. When some of the shippers had complained, Mexican soldiers had come, and a fort had been built at Velasco, where the Brazos River spilled into the Gulf waters.

In every town, every stagecoach stop, like Woods' Fort, Texans talked about the new laws and what could be done about them. No one had any real solutions. A lot of the men talked about doing violent things. These American frontiersmen, after all, had fought their way to this place, and would fight for their rights and freedoms if and when called upon.

Families like the Woods had been in such situations before. Zadock's father had fought at Bennington during the Revolution. Minerva's family, the Cottles of Vermont, had been among the first to head across the continent to settle the Missouri Territory. Minerva herself had bravely helped defend the town of Troy, Missouri, during the Black Hawk Wars, and had been hostess to Lieutenant Zachary Taylor and the United States Army during the War of 1812.

The Gonzales family had also endured the dangers of the new frontier of the Coahuila-Texas Province, the northern territory of the Republic of Mexico. Against Comanche raids and mercenaries, these Tejanos knew well the challenges facing families on the frontier. For ten years, Señor Gonzales and his family had fought the wilderness around them, taming a place they could call home, where children could be safe, and a business profitably worked. They, too, would be willing to stand strong against any who would restrain their dreams.

"Is Mr. Wilbarger coming through again soon, Pa?" Henry asked, interrupting the older men's conversation. Leander looked disapprovingly, but Zadock smiled at his youngest son.

"Don't know, son," he said, reaching over to muss the blond head of hair, "but if there's news, we're sure to hear about it. Ours is the last outpost this far to the west, but there's some who are building up across the Colorado. Word'll have to go everywhere once a decision's been made."

"Señor Woods," Antonio chimed in, "I know my padre will want to know. I hope you will tell us any news."

"No need to worry, young Antonio," Zadock replied. "We'll need every good man when the time comes." The old man gazed up into the sky, as if listening for some secret message in the noonday breezes. "It'll come," he said, almost in a whisper. "I feel it in these old bones of mine." He paused. The other three waited with respect for the next word.

"Like feeling the storm coming."

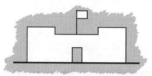

Chapter Seven

The first sign of the coming political storm arrived at Woods' Fort three weeks later, in the person of Strap Buckner.

"Henry!" Leander called from the cookhouse to his little brother. "Come quick! Strap Buckner is riding in!" The twenty-two-year-old Leander threw down the stewpot he had been scrubbing, wiped his hands on his homespun overalls, and took off in a sprint for the front entrance of the prairie fortress, Henry at his heels. Henry glanced up to the second floor of the structure, as their mother peeked from behind the leather portal covering. Leander pointed as he ran. "It's Cap'n Buckner, come with news!"

Zadock had told the family many stories about Aylett C. Buckner, who represented the perfect frontier soldier across the Texas boundaries. Tall and wide-shouldered, his nickname had come many years earlier as a comparison to "a strapping oak tree, bending but never breaking in the stormy winds." His exploits made for stories told at taverns and livery stables from Natchitoches to Brazoria.

When he had first arrived in Texas, Buckner and Stephen Austin had crossed swords in an argument over dealings with the Mexican government. Austin had preferred compromise and negotiation; Buckner was always in favor of fighting!

Now, however, in the tense times since the decree of 1830, Buckner had become a trusted ally of Austin's Colony, and a messenger to the citizens along the western edge of Texas. His arrival at any outpost or ranch meant the latest news, as well as an entertaining time for stories, true and otherwise.

By the time Henry caught up with his brother in the front yard of the fort, he saw Buckner and their father already in deep conversation, frowns on their faces. The two brothers slid to a stop in the dirt, and waited respectfully just within listening distance.

"Trouble at Anahuac," Captain Buckner explained. "The duties officer there has arrested three Texans, and everyone's hollering for action."

"What happened?" Zadock wanted to know the whole story before making any decision.

"Juan Davis Bradburn—that's the officer the Mexicans sent there—he's been stirrin' up the pot for a year now. Used to be the commandant of the presidio there, guarding the port." Buckner spit out the name as if it tasted bad. "Anyhow, when Colonel Austin convinced the government to get rid of the man who'd been there before, a no-account named Fisher, Bradburn just moved in and took on the whole operation. Been collecting taxes there and over at Velasco, too."

Zadock interrupted, "That's the law, the port duties. We all hate it, true enough, but what's that got to do with Bradburn?"

"Taking himself too seriously, if you ask me," Buckner smiled as he warmed to the story, "feeling pretty big for his britches! Throwing his authority around, pushing on folks up and down the coast. Anyhow, man named of Bill Travis and two others rode into Anahuac last week, that'd be the tenth of June, I reckon, to talk with Bradburn." Henry noticed that the big man grinned when he said, talk.

"Don't know Travis," remarked Zadock.

"Lawyer, they say. Just to Texas this year. Some say he's a loudmouth." He paused and glanced at Leander. "Should fit in around these parts!" Everyone chuckled. Henry nodded. He wanted Buckner to continue.

"Got into a shouting match, so I'm told. Bradburn just up and had 'em arrested, threw 'em in the jailhouse."

"What's Colonel Austin doing about it?" asked Henry, who risked interrupting the two adults, but neither seemed to mind.

"Trying to keep everyone calm," Buckner replied. "But it's not working. People been angry near two years about that law." He spat onto the ground for emphasis. "This may be the last straw."

"What's your message, Mr. Buckner?" Zadock wanted to get to the point of the big man's arrival here on the Colorado.

"Two things. Spreading the word that there's trouble on the coast. And asking if anyone wants to ride with me to Anahuac."

"Ride? What for?" Zadock frowned, ready as any man or woman on the frontier to defend his rights and his family. This sounded like the beginnings of a bigger confrontation than might be needed.

"Just in case, really," Buckner seemed to choose his words carefully, "in case there's more trouble. In case Bradburn doesn't release the men. If the garrison gets up in arms. Whatever . . ." He let the thought drift off in the dusty air.

Leander spoke up. "I'll go with you, Cap'n."

Zadock and Henry both looked sharply at him at the same time. Zadock stared into his son's eyes for a brief moment, then turned back to the visitor.

"What else can we do for you, sir? You're welcome to stay a bit, join us for a meal?"

Strap Buckner extended his right hand to the older man. "Thank you kindly, sir. I'd be much obliged. And if I could get your boy here," he motioned in Henry's direction, "to scrub down my horse, I'll be on my way this afternoon. Got some distance to go still."

The four turned almost in a military about-face at the same time and walked toward the dining area inside the fort's timbered walls. Zadock and Buckner continued to talk, in almost a whisper now. Henry strained but could not understand what they were saying. But he noticed the serious looks on their faces. They spoke of important decisions, he knew that much!

Minerva Woods set out the noon meal for the men, a lighter course than usual; it was too hot on these June days to heat a heavy meal in the middle of the day. The evening air made dining cooler and gave a better atmosphere for the breads and cakes that came from her baking oven. Today, the fare would be a pork and bean stew, cobs of fresh corn from the fields, and ale.

Henry and Leander chose a mug of goat's milk with their food.

During the conversation at the dining table, Zadock and Buckner decided that the men at Highsmith's Settlement would need to hear the news. That trip took Buckner out of his route, and Zadock volunteered to get the word to his old friends there.

Benjamin Highsmith and his family, Henry knew, had come to Texas at the same time as the Woods, in 1823. The group had met along the Mississippi River route that travelers often used coming from Missouri or the Ohio valley, and had journeyed overland to Natchitoches, in Louisiana. They had crossed the Sabine into Texas on Christmas Day, and, although they had taken different routes in the nine years since, stayed in touch by occasional trips to each other's homes.

Highsmith had eventually settled up the Brazos, on the north side of El Camino Real, the Mexican mission highway. This was in dangerous territory, too near Comanche hunting grounds, but several families had made their homes there, protecting one another and allowing others to settle in some safety down the river as well.

It would take a three days' ride from Woods' Fort, almost due north. Only the

Colorado River presented an obstacle to anyone traveling this route. The prairie spread evenly to the north, and a trail turning up along the Brazos River stayed well-worn from the wagons and horse traders who used it year-round.

Henry volunteered to make the trip to the Highsmith place, and jumped when his father gave his permission! Leander had chosen to accompany Buckner back to the coast, gathering recruits for a makeshift "army" headed to Anahuac. Zadock reluctantly decided to stay put: there was too much work around the fort for all of the men to be gone at the same time.

Zadock reminded everyone of the time, three years earlier, when the men had left for a three-day hunting trek. In their absence, Minerva and the several women who lived in the vicinity of the fort were left alone with the children. A band of roving Comanches had arrived at the fort early the second morning, led by the notorious Chief Buffalo Hump of the Penataka tribe. Fortunately, two head of beef turned out to be the only payment demanded by the Indians, and they had departed peacefully.

A second incident like that might not go as well. Zadock would stay this time.

By late afternoon, Buckner and Leander had ridden on, well-supplied with biscuits and pemmican in their saddlebags. Minerva had sneaked a bag of hard candy into her son's vest pocket as well.

Henry left soon after, headed for the Gonzales ranch, where he hoped Señor Gonzales would allow Antonio to accompany him to the Highsmith settlement.

Henry found not only a traveling companion, but supper and a night's bedding, too. The boys fell asleep still whispering excitedly about the great responsibility given to them by the leaders of the colony. Two hours before dawn, they awakened, dressed, and saddled their mounts for the journey. Señora Gonzales saw to it that a healthy breakfast of eggs and bacon started them on their way.

This would be an important ride! Perhaps Texas' future clung to the boys' success. At least, the two teens thought so as they rode from the ranch into the darkness, following for a little while the sparkling North Star.

Chapter Eight

On the journey to the Highsmith place, Antonio spotted the black-eared jackrabbit. The cagey prairie animal froze in place, trying very much to look like a stalk of brush. Jackrabbits very seldom crouch when they hide, preferring to remain motionless but in sight of the danger approaching.

Antonio pulled his palomino pony to a sudden stop, and, taking his slingshot from its pouch on his belt, bent far from the saddle in the direction of the two long ears standing erect twenty yards away. The high grass had concealed the rest of the prey, but he had done this hundreds of times before, aiming a well-polished stone selected from the pouch just inches below where the ears seemed to sprout.

Away went the stone, whistling through the air. Henry noticed the action and heard the zing of the weapon. His eyes quickly followed in the direction of the shot, just in time to see the ears disappear. The jack had dropped in its tracks!

Antonio dismounted, hitting the ground running, his pal only two strides behind. They reached the spot where the rabbit had been standing, and Antonio bent down to reach into the high grass.

That's when the jack, only stunned by the stone's glancing blow, decided to somersault to its feet. Its long, flat back feet came flipping suddenly up out of the grass, landing square on Antonio's face! The jackrabbit's legs, its strongest weapon, sent Tonio reeling back, his arms flailing in the air, his slingshot soaring off to his right.

The scared animal managed to right itself and take off in a blur through the grass. It disappeared in a matter of seconds, almost as if it had never been there at all!

Henry might, ordinarily, have taken off in hot pursuit, his own slingshot ready. But he laughed much too hard at his friend to consider the chase! The sight of that brown fur exploding up from the ground into Tonio's face and his compadre careening back in a silly cartwheel was too much.

Antonio sat up, his legs spread-eagled on the ground. He rubbed his nose and jaw, where a red welt had already begun to form. Henry laughed so hard that he thought he might burst. But the moment of pain from the attack had gone, and Tonio found himself giggling, too.

The two friends rolled on the ground for several minutes, pointing and chuckling at each other. A friendly wrestling match began, dust and grass flying through the air, and ended almost as soon as it had begun.

They had work to do, a mission to accomplish. No time for the silliness! It was time to ride on.

The boys arrived at Benjamin Highsmith's farmhouse on the afternoon of their third day on the trail. A gaggle of little children met them on the road in sight of the house. Travelers rarely came to this part of the Texas province and so always became a source of entertainment for the little ones as well as for news.

Mrs. Highsmith sent one of the children out to the fields to retrieve her husband and invited the boys in for water and rest. She knew Henry from previous visits and welcomed Antonio to her home. When Mr. Highsmith arrived, his wife took the several little ones still hanging around and excused herself to the cook house.

Henry relayed the message as calmly as he could to the older man, although he grew more excited as he talked. Mr. Highsmith had to ask Henry to slow down once to get the information clearly.

Henry and Antonio enjoyed the attention they received from the Highsmiths and others who joined the discussion later that evening. After a supper of cabrito and corn hash, everyone listened carefully to the options lined out by the elders. Some would ride immediately for Anahuac. However, it was much too dangerous this far up the Brazos to abandon the community and its families, so most of the men chose to stay. Word of a Comanche raiding party had come only the day before, and all of the frontier folks had gone on alert.

Henry allowed that they had not seen any sign of the Indians. He and Antonio accepted an invitation to stay overnight at the settlement. They would leave before daybreak, heading back for the Woods' Prairie community. The three men who had volunteered to head to the coast would leave at the same time as the boys, accompanying them several miles down the Brazos River trail, then splitting up to continue to the Old Atascosito Road and to Anahuac.

The meeting of the men and the two boys finally broke up around midnight. As the settlers filed out of the house and back to their homes, Antonio and Henry bedded down in Highsmith's barn. A long return trip home awaited them over the next three days. They would need a good night's sleep.

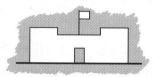

Chapter Nine

Antonio's father told many stories about El Camino Real, an ancient highway built by the early Spanish explorers to connect the missions built all across Texas. Most of it appeared now as no more than a rutted trail; stones along the road marked distance and direction. For a hundred years, settlers and soldiers had traveled this route, from deep in Mexico south of the Rio Grande, through San Antonio and to Nacogdoches and the old stone fort.

South and east of El Camino Real, Texans had come to live and work the frontier lands. North and west of the road, however, a dangerous "no-man's land" existed where few dared to explore. In that mysterious land lived the Comanche.

Henry's father had told him about the Comanches, originally a Plains tribe from far to the north, a nation of Native Americans pushed south by their enemies and as they followed the great bison herds. As the first natives on the continent to discover the horse, these fierce warriors owed their discovery to the Spanish conquistadores who left many horses to roam the plains in the 1550s.

Their expertise as riders on the plains widened the territory where they would rove, and enabled their raiding parties to escape into the hills and canyons high on the Canadian River.

Occasionally, Comanches roamed down across El Camino Real, seeking food and the plunder of Texas settlers, often taking young children who would become slaves of the Indian tribe. Men had been hired to protect Austin's colony and to range the borderlands of Texas, which included this old Spanish highway. Still others built small forts in this region as well, to serve as places for communities to gather in times of attacks. Woods' Fort had been one of the first built, back in 1828. Robbins' Fort stood along the Trinity River banks to the northeast, and Highsmith had built a barricade on his property in 1830. That same year, Fort Tenoxtitlan sprang up just south of Highsmith and several miles outside El Camino Real.

Henry Woods and Antonio Gonzales rode at an easy gait along the trail, headed south and west toward the Colorado River valley. They had left the three settlers several hours earlier, bidding them farewell and good fortune on their journey to Anahuac and whatever exciting adventures might await them there!

The boys knew the landmarks of this area well. Their conversation had trailed off as they rode, each rider lost in his own thoughts. Henry wondered if his brother Leander had reached Anahuac yet and what was going on there. Would there be fighting? Would Colonel Bradburn resist and call out his soldiers to meet the Texans?

Antonio spoke dreamily of Elisabeta. He had not seen her in more than two weeks, and he missed her a lot! Lisa, the daughter of Francisco and Maria Elinguam, had been his girlfriend ever since the community fiesta last Christmas. Her big black eyes seemed to float in his mind now, as he rode along the dusty road. He could hardly wait to get home and see her. Her family lived only a half-day's ride south of his ranch, a trip always worth the effort.

Antonio had just daydreamed of Lisa turning to him as he extended his hand to her, when Henry struck him on the shoulder! What?

"Tonio!" Henry whispered.

"Tonio!" Henry's voice urged. "Look there, to the right on the rise!" He pointed as the horses slowed.

Indians! Four rode slowly in the opposite direction of the boys, just over the hillock so that only their heads could be seen. They did not seem to have spotted the two travelers yet.

Without another word, both boys turned their mounts quickly to the left, off the main trail and into the ditch that ran alongside. Their horses' hooves splashed in the standing water. Henry rode in front now, using the reins to direct his horse up and out of the ditch. They clambered onto the prairie, increasing the gallop directly away from the potential danger.

Up ahead, a prickly pear grove connected the high grass with two long hedges of wild brush. The boys knew they would be safer on the other side of those wild shrubs, out of sight of the Indians. Antonio glanced quickly over his shoulder.

The Indians had gone! A glance in every direction came up blank. Had it been a mirage? No, they had seen them, all right. Perhaps they had just ridden on, down the other side of the hill and on their way. Still, frontier experience told them to continue on to the east until plenty of ground lay between them.

Ten minutes passed. The boys finally slowed down their mounts, resting but wary under the shade of a lone oak tree that stood beside the hedgerow. They did not dare even speak for the moment. Henry kept an eye to the north, while Antonio surveyed the prairie back west where they had left the trail.

Another fifteen minutes elapsed. Still no sign of danger. Henry spoke first, breaking the silence.

"I reckon it's safe. Let's head another mile east, then we'll take out for the river." Henry dug his heels into his mount, and the horse responded by lurching out from under the shade and onto the prairie. Antonio followed just behind, glancing again behind him every minute or so.

The two wary riders traveled less than a quarter-mile from the shade oak, when they realized, too late, what had become of the Indians. The raiding party had circled around behind the rise and directly into the path being traced by the boys.

Henry pulled hard on the reins and halted just a pace ahead of Antonio.

Now they counted five Indians, not the four they had spotted earlier. The Indians sat quietly on their ponies, facing the two teen-agers. Two held rifles casually in the crooks of their arms. The others brandished long, polished bows, and feathered arrows nicked into place, ready to fly.

The boys saw no expression on any of the burnished faces, nor any war paint visible at the distance that separated the two groups of riders. Three braves wore dark blue cotton shirts over buckskin breeches, and one of these had on what appeared to be a cowboy hat. The other two displayed beaded vests made of bone pieces and animal teeth hanging from their necks on leather thongs.

Antonio managed a whispered call. "Henry, make a run for it!" he urged.

"No, wait!" Henry raised his left hand at his friend. "We'd have no chance. Let's see what they want."

Henry took a deep breath, eased his horse forward two paces, and raised his right arm into the air in a salute. The Indian with the cowboy hat mirrored the boy's motion with his own, then lowered his rifle and rode closer. The others waited where they had stood.

"Hello," Henry said, and felt foolish not having anything better to say. He kept his arm raised, his hand open.

"Why do you ride here?" the group's apparent leader asked.

"We are on our way home," replied Henry, pointing with his right arm to the south. "We still have two days to ride."

"Follow us," the brave commanded without raising his voice.

Without waiting for the boys to respond, the five warriors wheeled their mounts in tandem, and started for the west, back in the direction of the Spanish trail. Henry glanced at Antonio, who shrugged as if to say, what choice do we have? The boys rode behind the Indians, lagging some twenty paces to the rear but without thought of escape, yet.

One of the small rises behind which the Indians must have ridden now loomed before them. At the top, Henry and Antonio could see El Camino Real in the distance and a pocket of elms and shrubs halfway between. Movement in the grove suddenly caught the boys' eyes. More Indians awaited! That meant more trouble for sure!

Antonio looked to his left, wondering if he could make a break for it now, and how far he might get. He deliberately dropped another several paces behind Henry, measuring each step as if to prepare for just the right moment to make his move.

Suddenly, a horse and rider bolted from the trees up ahead, making a dash right for them! He hollered something in his own language, as if signaling to the five braves, waving his left arm in the air as he clung with his right hand to his horse's mane.

Antonio sensed trouble. While the attacker distracted the Indians, he turned his palomino's head to the left, and dug his heels into its haunches.

"Henry!" he cried out. "Make a run for it! C'mon!"

Antonio looked over his shoulder for an instant. Henry's mount had leapt into action, but in the wrong direction! Henry headed right for the hard-riding Indian! The five braves turned their ponies out of his way as he closed the distance to the lone rider. Henry let out a wild whooping holler.

"Crooked Path!" Henry called out. "It's you!"

The Tonkawa boy raced for his friend with a wide grin on his face. As their horses met, the two boys clasped hands, nearly pulling each other to the ground.

What a relief, thought Henry. They had come upon a band of Tonkawas, not Comanches, traveling in the region not far from their village on Little River! And here rode his friend, whom he had saved weeks before after finding him bleeding from the arrow wound.

They spent the next hour catching up on getting to know each other better. Henry asked Crooked Path to come with him and Tonio as they returned to Woods' Prairie, hinting that they might head to the coast. Great adventures awaited them! But the Tonkawa boy declined. He had work to do with the other braves. They must hunt for food to take back to their village and would be at least another day on the trail.

Bidding farewell to the Indian party, Antonio and Henry finally mounted up and headed home, a last wave parting them from their new friend and ally.

The boys spent most of their journey home recounting their face-off with the Indians and a discussion of the possibility that riding for Velasco might be a great adventure indeed!

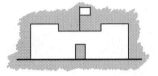

Chapter Ten

Antonio and Henry worked on the plan all the way home. Getting permission from their parents to make the long journey to the Gulf Coast would be tricky. Trouble brewed at Anahuac and Velasco. Leander Woods must certainly already be in the vicinity, having traveled east with Strap Buckner days earlier. The boys knew they might be away from home for as long as ten days, counting the ride across Austin's Colony and back.

It seemed like a simple plan. Antonio would ask his father while explaining that Henry's parents had already given their permission. At the same time, at Woods' Fort, Henry would repeat the same story. It amounted to only a small lie, they convinced each other. After all, they were men now, weren't they? They had been asked to take on the important mission of taking Captain Buckner's message to Highsmith's Settlement, which they had successfully accomplished. A trip east did not seem too much to ask.

When Antonio rode to say goodbye to Elisabeta, it did not go at all well! Lisa went from being sad to being angry. Then, she seemed to not care at all what Tonio did with himself! Confused now, Tonio had imagined that his girlfriend would hug him and encourage this brave venture. She would wish him well and promise to think about him while he was away. Perhaps she might shed a tear for her "hero."

Instead, Lisa folded her arms, turned away from him, and stiffened her lower lip in a pouty expression.

"Go on, then," she finally blurted out, "go away with your friend, go away and be killed and never come back. I don't care."

"Lisa," Antonio struggled to find the right fiwords, "I will come back. I promise. We won't be gone long. You'll see." None of the words seemed constructive.

After the silent treatment had dragged on, Antonio reluctantly rode away from Elisabeta's ranch. At first, she did not seem to notice that he'd gone. But the last time Antonio looked back, he saw her turn toward him and wave. He gladly returned her wave, and spurred his horse on, feeling only a little less confused.

★ ★ ★

No one west of Brazoria could bake like Henry's mother! Girding up the strength to tell his parents about the plan, Henry found himself temporarily distracted by one of the best meals he had ever eaten!

Fresh venison had been cooked over the charcoal fire, and cobs of corn just off the stalk soaked in churned butter. Minerva had baked bread along with her famous wild raspberry pie, and the wonderful smells mixed and filled the dining room of the tavern inside the fort's walls.

The family conversation remained lively longer than usual. Even Henry's two oldest brothers, Norman and Monte, had come for supper. Norman's wife, Jane, helped at the cookhouse, while Monte and Betsy watched over their three children. Betsy, expecting another baby soon, could not chase down the little ones as easily as usual. Henry helped, engaging his niece and two nephews in a game of chase out in the yard until the supper bell sounded.

There would be no meals like this one on their journey, Henry thought to himself as he ate. Henry knew all he needed to survive on the trail, but there would be no berry pies, hot and juicy and bittersweet.

Still, if the adventure meant anything to him, it meant some sacrifice. Texas' future lay at stake!

★ ★ ★

Sharing the separate conversations later, Henry and Antonio expressed surprise that their fathers had said almost exactly the same thing when the question came up!

"Henry," Zadock Woods had looked at his youngest son seriously, "I think your going on this trip makes a good deal of sense."

"But Tonio's father," Henry had started to say, then realized what his father had just said! "You really think so, Pa?"

"Yes, I do. You are a young man now, and it's fitting that you be a part of what is happening in Texas these days. This is the Texas you will grow up in, and where you will be a leader someday. Find Leander as soon as you can, and stay close to him and Cap'n Buckner. You'll be fine."

At the Gonzales ranch, the conversation had been longer, but with the same result. Señor Gonzales asked many questions of his only son, but Antonio's mother quietly began packing items into a bag for her son to take with him. She recognized the significance of this decision: Antonio had grown up. The time had arrived for such a journey.

Both boys agreed that time could not be wasted now that their plan had been accepted, and without having to lie. Hasty goodbyes said all around, a firm handshake between fathers and sons signaled the first step of this new adventure. In a last wave goodbye, the two young "soldiers" had started off together for the cause of Texas!

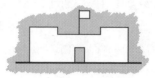

Chapter Eleven

The first leg of the journey covered the roads from Woods' Fort to San Felipe, the capital of Austin's Colony. The trip was an easy three-day ride, following an east-west path on the other side of the Colorado River, crossing the Atascosito Road and on to the Brazos River trail. A ferry landing had been built several years before to cross the Brazos here, and Stephen F. Austin had located his empresario headquarters and home alongside the crossing.

The two boys spotted Colonel Austin's home first, constructed of logs and typical of the early frontier cabins. Two large living areas, each with its own fireplace, resided under one shingled roof separated by a walk-through space they called a "dog-run." A large porch jutted out on the front of the cabin, and a cookhouse and outhouse sat off to themselves around back.

The cabin looked abandoned. Mr. Austin must be on his way to Anahuac, the boys decided.

But plenty of other Texans walked about the small town. Some may have thought San Felipe small, although Henry remembered only Moore's Landing east of his own community as being any larger. Antonio, on the other hand, had made two trips with his family to San Antonio de Bexar. Along with Nacogdoches, up to the northeast, San Antonio had grown to be the largest community in the Coahuila-Texas province.

San Felipe de Austin, the colony capital, boasted a livery stable, a smithy, two general merchandise stores, and the only newspaper office in Texas! A tavern, a small inn, and another dozen or so log cabin homes sat scattered along the river bank and out onto the rolling prairie.

The boys headed first to the newspaper office. This would be the best place to get the latest information, except perhaps for the tavern.

Henry and Antonio tied their mounts to a post in front of one of the general stores and crossed the dusty street to a small building with a sign painted above its door: TEXAS GAZETTE.

The door squeaked as they pushed it open. Inside the office, a shaft of light from the single window to the right of the door left shadows in most of the room.

Henry paused to let his eyes adjust to the shadows. Two men stood over by a large desk, talking quietly with one another. One of the men, the taller of the two, had long, white hair, brushed back to reveal a pair of spectacles residing on the bridge of his nose.

The other man, not much taller than Henry, wore a dark suit and appeared to carry a crutch under his right arm. He stood slightly bent over, which forced him to look up at an awkward angle as he spoke to his companion. Henry suddenly realized he knew the shorter man.

"That's Three-Legged Willie," Henry whispered to Antonio, just closing the door behind them.

"Who is he, a pirate?"

"No," Henry shook his head, "he's a Texan, a friend of my Pa's. He came to the fort last winter."

The two boys walked up to the two men, who finally turned to look at them. The taller man spoke first.

"Can I help you boys?" His voice had an odd twang to it.

"Yessir," Henry spoke up. "My name's Henry Woods. This here's Antonio Gonzales. We're from Woods' Prairie." Henry stuck out his right hand.

"Pleased to meet you boys," the taller man continued. He shook Henry's hand, then

Antonio's. "I'm Gail Borden, editor of the paper. This is my friend . . ."

"Three-Legged Willie!" Henry blurted.

". . . Robert Williamson," Borden finished his introduction with a smile. The shorter man grinned widely as he motioned toward the boys.

"You're right, son," Williamson said, "Three-Legged Willie is what they call me around here." He spoke with a slow Georgia drawl.

The boys stood politely as the men finished their conversation. Henry recalled a story that he had heard at the fort about the newspaper that had come to Texas. Gail Borden, a New Yorker, had come to Texas as a surveyor for Austin's Colony but had gotten involved in the newspaper business with Godwin Cotten in San Felipe. Their TEXAS GAZETTE had run for a year and just closed down that spring. Borden was looking for backers to start another paper.

Henry knew all about the other man. Robert McAlpin Williamson was only twenty-six, and already involved in the politics and commerce of Texas. He was one of the many who had migrated from Georgia in the past two years. His distinctive handicap went unnoticed by those who knew him, for Three-Legged Willie never let his condition slow him down.

"You're Zadock Woods' son?" Williamson asked. Henry nodded eagerly. "A good man, your pa. Been on the frontier all his life. How's your ma?"

"Just fine, thank you." Henry remembered his manners. "We've come looking for my brother Leander. Have you seen him, sir?"

The two men glanced at one another. Borden shook his head. "No one by that name that I recall. Robert?"

"No, haven't seen him since last December, when I dined with you, Henry."

Antonio perked up. "We're following him and Cap'n Buckner. They left last week for the coast. Heard there was trouble."

Williamson smiled again. "You come to help out, is that right?"

"Yessir," Antonio replied. He tried to stand a little taller.

"Well, men," Borden interrupted, "got bad news for you, I'm afraid. We just heard that the flap over at Anahuac is done. No trouble after all. Just a lot of shouting."

The two boys' shoulders drooped at the same time. What discouraging news! No trouble after all! They'd even missed the shouting.

"What about the tax collector? And the men who were arrested?" Henry pressed.

"Bradburn was relieved of his duties. Fired by the Mexican government. He'd been causing trouble for a year. The Texans were released before the mob even arrived." Borden reported as if preparing an article for his newspaper.

"Some of them expected back today," Williamson chimed in. "Captain Russell is due back by evening, I heard."

"Captain Russell?" Antonio asked.

"Bill Russell—owns a sloop that he sails up the Brazos to Bell's Landing these days. Came through here the other day on his way to Anahuac to join the others. Said he had to be back to the boat by the 25th. That's tomorrow." Three-Legged Willie seemed to be finished with the news report. He shifted his weight on to the crutch, grabbed a felt hat off the desk and pulled it down over his forehead.

"See you, gentlemen," he nodded at each of them. He and Borden shook hands briefly, and the crippled man moved toward the door.

Antonio, closest to the door, opened it for him. As Williamson marched by, Antonio looked down. The crutch carried the weight of Willie's right leg, bent permanently back at the knee. The man's trouser leg wrapped around a withered ankle, and what looked like a leather slipper covered the small foot.

Williamson crossed to the office porch and ambled down the walk. He moved smoothly and confidently from many years of managing on a crutch. He nodded a hello to several people he passed. Antonio stared after him until the man had turned a corner and disappeared.

Henry, meanwhile, continued the conversation with Mr. Borden.

Over a hundred Texans had gathered at San Felipe the week before, apparently including Leander. Most had headed for Anahuac to confront Bradburn. Another group had ridden on to Bell's Landing, presumably on their way to the fort at Velasco, at the mouth of the Brazos. Borden didn't remember who had led the second party, but he thought Strap Buckner had been in that group.

Henry knew that wherever Cap'n Buckner went, Leander would follow. Perhaps an adventure awaited them after all!

With a round of handshakes, the boys left Mr. Borden and the newspaper office. They loped across the street to their horses.

"I'm starving!" Antonio rubbed his stomach. "Let's get some supper, Henry."

"All right. But then, we need to figure out our next step. We have to get to Velasco. WE HAVE TO FIND LEANDER!"

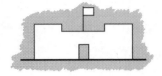

Chapter Twelve

The arrival of the first men back from Anahuac interrupted the boys' meal. Riding into San Felipe from the northeast, seven Texans made their way to the tavern amid a growing crowd hurling questions at them from every direction.

The men tried to answer the questions while, at the same time, heading for a long-over-due meal. They looked tired and dusty from the long ride from Anahuac.

Captain Russell strode into the tavern first. The boys watched him across the dining room, eating his food much faster than the others, in a hurry to continue on, they guessed correctly. Before Henry and Antonio even had the chance to make their way through the crowd to speak to him, Russell had made his apologies to the others at the table and excused himself, walking quickly through the swinging doors and to the livery stable.

Without a word, the boys left the tavern, mounted their horses and headed at an easy gait for the stables, catching up with Russell just as he paid the stable boy for scrubbing down his horse.

"Cap'n!" Henry called, as they rode up to where the tall Texan stood.

William Russell turned at the sound and smiled in the direction of the two riders who had halted at his side.

"What can I do for you boys?" he asked easily.

"Well, sir," Antonio began, "my name's Antonio Gonzales, and this is Henry Woods. We're headed for Bell's Landing, and were hoping you might be going that way." The Tejano teenager leaned from his saddle and extended his right hand to the man.

"Nice to meet you boys," Russell replied. "This is your lucky day, I reckon. Bell's Landing is right where I'm headed. You're welcome to join me. I always appreciate the company."

Without another word, Russell climbed onto his large black steed, nodded to the stable boy standing off to one side, and urged his mount out on to the main street. The boys looked quickly at each other, smiled, and took off after him.

The three traveled without conversation for the first several miles. The sun drifted down to the horizon at their backs, and the air began to cool. The evening star sprang to life in the azure sky, and Henry remembered to make a silent wish on it, as his mother had instructed him years before.

When they did speak, the three concluded that it seemed a mighty fine evening, and Texas a great place to be on nights like this. Captain Russell indicated that they might ride as far as Mrs. Powell's tavern, where they would put up for several hours until heading on long before dawn.

Russell spoke briefly about the encounter at Anahuac. There had been no real confrontation between the Texans and Bradburn's garrison of soldiers. Orders had already been sent, relieving the tax collector of his command only hours before the "investigating party" (that's what Russell called his group) had arrived.

The Texans had immediately released the three men. In addition to the lawyer Bill Travis, Sam Allen and Patrick Jack had expressed their gratitude on being rescued. Mr. Jack, a name Henry thought sounded familiar, had made a brief speech to the gathered crowd, urging Texans to unite against the "tyranny of the

Mexican administration." Russell relished the phrase as if he were enjoying a piece of hard candy.

The tavern on the Brazos loomed out of the darkness, cutting off the conversation for the moment. The road-weary travelers dismounted, introduced themselves to the proprietress of the popular inn, and quickly bedded down in a back room. This would be a short night's sleep, with a busy day ahead.

Two hours before first light, Captain Russell gently shook the boys awake. They put up their bedrolls and accepted steaming hot mugs of black coffee from Mrs. Powell before leaving the hostel.

They had made a good fifteen miles before the dawn announced the new day. Traveling at an easy gait, they felt a purpose in the horses' strides. The trail from the inn left the Brazos at this point, making straight across a sometimes swampy flatland to Bell's Landing. There, Captain Russell's river schooner would be waiting.

Henry Woods recognized this land as familiar territory. Before building the fort out west, the Woods family had first settled here in the Brazoria area, along the San Bernard River bottoms just south and west of the landing where they now headed. Zadock and Minerva had started a small inn on the "league and labor" of land they had purchased as part of Austin's "Old 300" colonists.

From 1824, when Henry was only six years old, and for the next two years, a small community had grown up around Woods' Inn. Zadock and his sons, Norman and Leander, had surveyed the area for a township, lining out a square of streets running perpendicular and just off Old Caney Creek.

Henry remembered the days of exploring this coastal flatland, fishing with his brothers in the several streams on their property. He recalled the narrow escape from the jaws of a craggy old alligator when he was seven. Gosh, he hadn't thought of that in years! This had been a wonderful place to live, and what a surprise for all of the family when Pa had announced their move west to help Mr. Austin by building a fort on the Colorado River prairie!

Henry had not been back to this area since and now enjoyed some of the fond memories as he rode with the others this cool June morning. He smelled a hint of rain in the air and looked up to see billowy white thunderheads forming on the horizon. Could be a storm coming up today, he decided to himself.

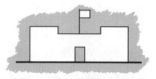

Chapter Thirteen

Henry remembered that his father had called Josiah Bell's boat landing the best one in Texas. The Brazos River had already become one of the primary routes for commerce into Austin's Colony even then. Commerce flowed on the Brazos except in the early spring when the flooded river ran too rough, and in late summer when drought conditions sank the river to a trickling stream. Crossing the Brazos was important to settlers and businessmen moving up and down the Gulf Coast plains.

Toward the coast from Bell's ferry, the community of Brazoria had sprung up in the last few years. Where the Brazos spilled into the salt-water gulf, Velasco and the fort stood out on the white-sand beach.

Travel along this stretch of the Brazos River was always busy. Henry, Antonio and Captain Russell arrived late in the morning at the boat landing. The two boys remained on their horses as the man with them strode over to the dock where a twenty-five-foot sailing vessel floated peacefully.

"AHOY THERE!" Captain Russell hailed from the riverbank. A broad-shouldered black man appeared from below deck.

"Is that you, Cap'n?" the lone crew member shouted back.

"Course it's me, Jeremiah. Wake up now! We need to be under way before noon." Russell walked along the dock impatiently and leaped gracefully onto the deck of his ship.

"Yessir, Cap'n," Jeremiah drawled. "Be ready for you in a jot." The man reached up to the mainsail rope just above his head. His burly arms began to work the ropes expertly.

Antonio and Henry watched all of this scene unfold as they sat on horseback.

"Henry," Antonio finally spoke up, "ask Captain Russell if we can come along. He's headed for Velasco for sure. That's where your brother's gonna be."

"I know, I know," Henry said. "That's sure faster than riding the trail." He paused. "CAP-TAIN!" he cried out.

Russell looked up from his work.

"Captain, can we join your crew? We want to come with you!"

Russell dropped the heavy rope to the deck and put his hands on his hips. He looked at the boys for just a moment.

"I'm afraid I can't do that, son," he said. "I have three other deckhands already hired on. They'll be here shortly. Besides," he continued, "it may be too dangerous. Not sure I want to be responsible for something happening to you."

Antonio gave Henry a look of discouragement and shrugged his shoulders.

"But Captain," Henry pressed, "we'll be all right. Won't make any trouble. We'll stay out of the way. Please, sir!"

Russell smiled as if he understood the boy's concern.

"Sorry, son. Best you stay here, though. Now excuse me. Got a lot of work to do, rigging up." Russell turned away.

"What'll we do, Henry?" Antonio frowned as he spoke.

"We're going," Henry offered after a moment. "Let's take the horses to the livery. C'mon!" He dug his heels into his mount, and the horse jumped into action. Antonio followed with a look of puzzlement on his face.

They rode quickly to the north side of the ferry, where a small stable had been set up. Henry gave the liveryman a half-dollar to put up the two horses and promised to return in a couple of days. With Tonio a step behind, Henry headed back toward Russell's dock.

"Henry, what're you doing? Captain said we couldn't go along."

"We're going, Tonio." Henry had a grim look on his face. "It's just that Cap'n Russell doesn't know he's gonna have passengers!"

Henry broke into a trot, and the two teens covered the short distance running until they reached the small dockhouse on the bank.

Peeking around its edge, the boys saw Russell and four other men on the ship deck, working in tandem to prepare the sails for the trip to Velasco. On the foredeck, a large brown canopy covered a bulky object that Henry had not noticed there before.

"There," Henry pointed. "We'll hide under that cover as soon as we get the chance." Antonio nodded. He still had a frown of wonder on his face.

Ten minutes passed. Russell shouted something to his crew, and three of the men followed the captain off the deck and back in the direction of the ferry. The two boys ducked behind the small shack as the men passed a few feet away.

The man left behind looked like the same one who had been there when they had first arrived. As soon as Russell had disappeared over the levee ridge, the man stepped to the aft deck, lay down on his back and closed his eyes. In less than a minute, Antonio thought he could hear the man snoring.

"Now!" Henry whispered urgently. He scrambled down the bank, crept along the dock and onto the ship, Antonio at his elbow. In four quick, quiet strides they reached the canopy. They slid underneath the heavy tarp and lay on their stomachs, stretched out as best they could in the cramped quarters. Antonio could see the deck of the ship through a small tear in the cover.

Not two minutes later, they heard the sounds of voices, and Antonio saw four figures coming down the dock.

Russell began to bark orders, startling the sleeping crewman. Everyone now bent to the task of getting underway. The mainsail went up as the ropes loosened from the dock moorings. Russell stood at the huge steering wheel in the center of the ship, calling out instructions every few seconds. The others jumped at every order.

The ship moved cautiously away from the dock and out into the swift currents of the river. A breeze had just come up moments before, and now it tugged at the sails.

Antonio peered through the peephole of the tear. The dock grew smaller as the ship moved down the Brazos and then disappeared as the boat turned a bend in the river.

Neither boy even considered saying anything for the time being, although from their hiding place they would not have been heard by the crew. Henry had no idea how long the trip might take. He had watched barges on the Colorado around Moore's Landing before, but this vessel headed for a place Henry had never been. He settled down on the hard deck in the darkness.

Antonio kept an eye on the deck and Captain Russell, who seldom moved away from the wheel for the next hour. Three of the deckhands could be seen every now and then, walking near the canopy. The other man must have been below deck.

As the second hour came and went, Antonio heard his friend breathing in a steady count, sleeping soundly! For the first time since the two had crept into this secret place, Antonio looked around him. Only a tiny sliver of light from the torn peephole allowed him to see anything at all. He could barely make out part of Henry's form, stretched out four feet away.

In-between the boys, something—whatever the canopy covered—sat on two wooden wheels. It looked black and about a yard in length. Antonio reached carefully up and touched the object. It felt rough-textured and metallic. Antonio's hand fell back to his side. A cannon!

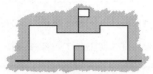

Chapter Fourteen

"CAP'N!" The shout caught both boys by surprise, as the black crew member pulled back the canopy that had been their hiding place.

Henry had been sleeping and thought the scream had come from a nightmarish creature exploding into his dream. The monster shook him so hard with its tentacles that he thought his teeth would come loose!

"Stop!" Henry cried as he woke at the same instant.

"Henry, it's me!" Antonio said, shaking him. Henry looked up. Antonio had a wild look in his eyes. In the background behind his friend loomed a giant shape. It was the crew member, hollering in his own moment of surprise having discovered the two stowaways.

"What is it, Jeremiah?" Russell's voice carried from aft of the ship.

"Come quickly, sir." Jeremiah reached down and grabbed a handful of Antonio's britches at the waist. He lifted the boy as if he were a sack of coffee beans and deposited him again on the deck to one side. Henry stood up, shaking his head to wake himself up.

"Well, what have we here, Jeremiah?" The commander smiled as he recognized his secret passengers. "Why, if it isn't my two young traveling companions! H'lo, boys!"

"Captain Russell, I can explain," Henry began.

"Never mind, son." Russell stopped him by raising one hand. "No explanation necessary. It's fairly obvious what's going on here, isn't it?" He furrowed his brow in Henry's direction.

Henry looked a bit sheepish, having been caught so easily. "Sorry, Captain," was all he could think to say. Antonio nodded his own apology.

"I understand, son," Russell said after a pause. "I just wish I could let you go on with us. But I just wouldn't feel right if something were to happen to either of you boys. Jeremiah!"

"Yessir, Cap'n," the big black man straightened his shoulders in an informal salute.

"Lower the mainsail and put these boys off yonder. We're just past Peach Point. They can walk back there and find something to eat." Russell turned back to the boys. "You boys know how to swim?"

"Yes, sir," both boys answered at the same time.

"Good enough, then," Russell pointed over the portside. "You'll likely only get your feet wet. Get up on that bank there, and walk back about a half-mile. There's a tavern in Peach Point. Tell the innkeeper Captain Russell says to feed you and put you up."

"But, sir," Henry began.

"Where are your mounts?"

"Back at Bell's Landing, sir. We put them up at the livery," Antonio spoke up.

"Well," Russell thought a moment, staring back upriver. "It's a pretty good hike from Peach Point. You could walk it, I suppose, in a day."

"Why can't we come along with you?" Antonio didn't relish a day's walk anywhere. "We won't cause you any trouble."

"Sorry, son. You're brave enough, both of you, just getting this far. But this is the end of the line for you. See you boys. Good luck."

And with that, the captain turned on his heel and walked back to the wheel. Jeremiah escorted the boys to the left side of the small deck.

The ship began to slow, as the mainsail shuddered down the mast. Russell steered to his left as close to the bank as he dared, still leaving about fifty feet of water for the stowaways to clear.

There seemed no choice, and Henry made the first move. With a last glance in Russell's direction, the teen-ager dived into the cool swirling waters of the Brazos, surfacing with a strong stroke just as his friend splashed into the water behind him. A dozen strokes more and Henry could feel his feet touch the muddy bottom of the river. He stood up and swaggered through the shallows onto the bank, just a step ahead of Antonio.

They sat on the bank to catch their breath, watching the sloop in full sail again moving down the middle of the river. They thought they saw the big black man waving from the aft deck as the ship disappeared around a bend. And then it was gone.

Henry and Antonio sat for several minutes where they had swum ashore, feeling the warming June sun dry their shirts and britches. The breeze drifted down the river with the current, and, up above, a flock of gray and white gulls wheeled below a lone cloudbank that drifted across the afternoon sky.

"Let's go," Henry finally spoke. "It's a good walk back to Peach Point, I reckon." He picked himself up, straightened his still soggy clothes and started up the bank. Antonio scrambled up after him. They stood at the edge of a flat prairie. Even from this vantage point, they could see nothing in any direction, except coastal grass bending like waves in the wind.

"Henry Woods, are you telling me that we're quitting?" Tonio couldn't believe his ears. "We're close, really close! It might be faster to the coast than back upriver." He let the thought trail off. Henry stared at him.

"You think so?" A smile creased his face.

"Sure I do," Antonio replied eagerly. "This is why we came this far. We can't go back now! We need to find Leander!"

"You bet, Tonio," Henry kicked a small stone down the bank and watched it ripple the waters. "Let's get going!"

The two companions launched themselves along a deer trail that followed the river south. They had a little extra bounce in each step now: the adventure was still on.

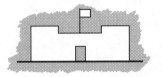

Chapter Fifteen

Henry William Munson had built a great plantation in Brazoria soon after the arrival of Austin's Old 300 colonists. His land stretched from the Brazos River near Peach Point north and east for thousands of acres. Near the center of this vast prairie ranch he had built a Georgian style mansion, complete with Greek pillars along the front and a curling staircase inside that led to the many rooms upstairs.

A barn and corral lay out in the back. Another quarter-mile away, a shanty town for the slaves housed over thirty men, women, and children who worked for Munson.

Munson had become one of the wealthiest men of Texas and a supporter of Texas causes as well.

On this June afternoon, Munson had converted his front yard into a campground and marching field for one hundred fifty Texans gathered there. These men had answered the call for help at Velasco, led by John Austin, the empresario's cousin. With Austin, in the forefront of the company, served William Wharton, Henry Smith and Thomas Westall. For spiritual guidance, Reverend J. W. Cloud had volunteered his services.

Noticeably absent, but expected to be involved, Captain William Russell had sent a message ahead that he would be sailing to the mouth of the Brazos and, more importantly, that he had a cannon on board. This news had been met with a great cheer by the company.

There, in all of his frontier gear, stood Strap Buckner, Colonel Austin's messenger and renowned soldier, with his new young friend, Leander Woods, whom he introduced to many of the others who had ridden in together during the day.

A simple plan had taken shape: Captain Austin would lead the troops to the vicinity of the fort at Velasco, where a demand for surrender of arms would be delivered. Meanwhile, Russell's schooner would be positioned within cannon range of the fort out on the Brazos River. In case of trouble, the force had been divided into three companies and a basic strategy for attack drawn up.

No one truly expected trouble, for the news of Bradburn being relieved of duty in Anahuac had calmed everyone's nerves. On the other hand, the men who had come with Wharton seemed eager for something to happen: they had come a long way and were itching for a fight!

At three o'clock in the afternoon, the Texas force rode out from Munson's place, headed for Velasco.

★ ★ ★

At three-thirty, Antonio and Henry walked onto the mansion yard, weary from their hike and disappointed to learn from a manservant that they had missed the war party.

The news would not deter either boy, however. Antonio and Henry had resolved they would see this adventure through, no matter the consequence. Pausing only long enough for a healthy drink of cool water, the two set out quickly, following the worn trail of over thirty horses that had just covered the prairie to the south.

Two hours later, the boys sighted the first sign of the Texans on the move. A cloud of dust and sand seemed to be rising on the horizon ahead of them, indicating the presence of horses stirring up the beach along the coast. The boys still had a couple of hours of hiking ahead of them, but now the trail at their feet and the cloud up ahead gave them a fresh new confidence that they had not come along too late.

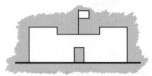

Chapter Sixteen

"There!" Antonio said, the first to spot the riders. Three men on horseback galloped hard from the north, heading for the same cloud of sand that the boys had set their sights on earlier. Probably Texans, Henry thought to himself as he looked where his friend pointed.

"I see 'em, amigo," Henry answered. "We're on the right trail for sure!" The boys broke into a trot, pacing each other over the now uneven terrain.

The flat river bottom prairie had given way to the marshy coastal plain. Up ahead, grass-covered dunes swayed on the horizon. Heavy cloud banks soared high above the gulf waters, indicating a forecast for night rains. Behind them, the sun began its final descent below the horizon. The runners' shadows stretched far ahead of them, winning the race to the beach.

The ground became gradually soggier now. The matted marsh vines wove a bizarre pattern beneath their feet. Frogs leaped out of their way, and at least twice Antonio spotted the silver-black backsides of water moccasins slithering off the trail.

Movement just ahead! What looked like disconnected heads rolling on top of the dunes momentarily stumped the two runners. Ten fast paces later, they saw the rest of the bodies, some on horseback, others walking about on the edge of the beach.

They had caught up with the Texans. Henry and Antonio kept their steady trot, still breathing easily, only five minutes away now. Looking past the troops, the boys now spotted the fort for the first time. It seemed no more than a mirage at first, the edges of the distant picture wavering in the heat's illusion. Still, the sight amazed them.

The Velasco stockade had been hastily assembled back in 1830, when the new laws took effect in Texas. The Mexican government feared resistance to the new customs duties to be collected, and had ordered a contingent of soldiers to Anahuac and Velasco. Ships that entered or left the Brazos River were required to stop at Velasco and report to the duties officer.

Under Juan Davis Bradburn's command, the ships had also been forced to travel a hundred miles out of their way to report again at the Anahuac station. This predicament had caused

Travis and the others to argue with Bradburn back in May. And it was that argument that had gotten them arrested, and had started up this whole reaction across the province.

The fort itself had been built a thousand yards up the beach from the gulf waters, and only a hundred yards or so from the Brazos River itself.

The fort was round and built up two stories high. A walkway circled the top of the walls, and one wide gate enclosed the fort's entrance. The gate faced directly toward the river. Above the entryway, tied down upon a parapet, sat a cannon. Any ship daring to run the river without registering first could be shot and sunk by the single piece of artillery.

Earlier in the year, Mexican troops under the command of Colonel Domingo Ugartechea reinforced the presidio on the beach, and now some two hundred soldiers manned the fortress and its firepower.

Now, the Texan forces intended to demand the surrender of the garrison!

As Henry and Antonio drew closer to the scene, they noticed three dramatic things taking place at the same time.

The Texans had formed into three distinct companies, arranging themselves in ordered lines at the shouted commands of several mounted officers. Antonio spotted the horses of these soldiers tethered to one side. All of the men, except their leaders, were on foot, armed with rifles and pistols, readying themselves for a march across the beach to the fort.

Up ahead, Henry could see what at first looked like ants scurrying about atop the mirage. The Mexican troops were moving into position on the fort's walkway, their muskets lined evenly along the wall. At least four, now five, soldiers marched behind the riflemen, probably giving orders of their own. At least one of the Mexicans brandished a saber, its blade catching the last of the sun's rays in flashes of light.

Approaching the dunes themselves now, the boys crawled through the slippery sand to the top and looked out over the scene.

"Look, Henry," Antonio whispered, although he wasn't sure why he needed to be quiet. "On the river!"

Henry had already seen it. Captain Russell's ship rolled easily on the waves that mixed gulf saltwater with the river's freshwater here at the mouth. The sailing vessel, its mainsail down, lay positioned directly in front of the fort's closed entrance. The cannon with which the boys had hidden earlier in the day now stood astride the portside deck, aimed at the Mexicans' artillery like its mirrored reflection.

At the exact moment that the ship caught Henry's gaze, a puff of blue smoke exploded from the cannon. Seconds later, the resounding BOOM! of the first shot echoed across the sand and startled the boys for an instant.

A shout went up from the Texans down on the beach and, at a command, the three companies began to move out from the edge of the dunes and onto the flat sands.

Henry now could see that the company on the right carried a large object with them, dragging it behind them with leather or vine thongs attached. It looked like a huge raft! Henry looked puzzled. What could they want with a raft in the middle of a battle?

Before any answer came to him, the much larger sound of gunfire spread like the evening shadows over the entire scene. Smoke enveloped the walkway of the fort in the distance, and three Mexican soldiers reloaded their cannon after having fired its first shot at the schooner. Antonio thought he saw two of the ship's crew scrambling across the foredeck. Had the cannon shot been true to the mark? Was the sailer damaged?

The darkness seemed to be hurrying across the spectacle now. The boys slid down the dunes and came to their feet in a dead run. The companies in the center and on the left had now moved to within fifty yards of the fortress. Men were diving to the ground, firing their rifles up at the Mexican defenders while at the same time seeking any bit of cover available on the beach.

What an enormous sound enveloped the scene! Hundreds of firearms, and two cannon, leveling deadly bullets in all directions. Off to his left, Antonio watched in horror as two Texans fell to the ground at almost the same moment, one grabbing for his shoulder, the other throwing both arms high in the air as he dropped.

Still the boys ran on into the fray, using the last of the daylight to make their way closer to the fort.

They could hear the shouted orders of the Texan officers very clearly now, for the boys had managed to catch up with the right flanking company. Some forty men had made their way only yards from the entrance to the fort, still dragging the strange object behind them.

Leander! Henry spotted his brother just off to the right of the raft-thing, bending down with two other men to help lift the heavy object up on its end. Others joined the effort, dropping their rifles in the sand for an instant or handing them to fellow soldiers.

Henry ran so fast that he literally bumped into his brother hard enough to knock both of them to the soft ground.

"Leander!" Henry shouted in the middle of the confusion. The older Woods boy shook his head as if to clear his view of the person nearly fallen on top of him.

"Little Brother!" Leander exclaimed. He wrapped his arms around his brother's shoulders and gave him a big bearhug. "What are you doing? Where did you—!" The terrible sound of gunfire from directly above them interrupted the conversation. Leander twisted around on top of Henry, shielding him from the bullets whizzing into the ground around them.

Another body rolled into them. Antonio, groping in the near-total darkness for his companion, had found them.

"We've come to help out!" Henry screamed into his brother's ear above the din. "It's Tonio!" He pointed at his friend with his free arm: he was still pinned to the beach by his brother's weight.

"Plenty to do!" shouted Leander as he rolled off Henry and pulled him to his feet behind the wooden breastworks that now stood on its end. The raft that the boys had seen had become a huge ladder to be lifted against the fortress wall. It now stood almost in position just below the Mexican cannon placement. The Texans had noted earlier, as Henry now saw, that the cannon would be ineffective close-in because it could not be bent at such an angle to cause any damage to those who could reach the gate.

Suddenly, off to their left, near the base of the wall beyond the entry gate, a tall Texas soldier had been the first to reach the garrison. He twisted into a position to fire right up the side of the escarpment. Looking down from atop the wall, several Mexican soldiers now leaned over the edge to return his fire. Their faces could not be seen in the darkness except as the flash of the muskets gave off an eerie light to silhouette them.

But everyone close enough to the scene on the ground knew the Texan. Strap Buckner, the old Indian fighter himself, had made it to the wall first. No one proved any braver than this frontiersman.

Shots rang out! One of the Mexican soldiers above screamed as he dropped his musket and clutched his face, keeling backward out of view from below. Someone next to Henry yelled, causing him to glance quickly to his left.

Strap Buckner had lowered his rifle and stood frozen in place facing the wall. Almost in slow motion, the rangy soldier turned until he seemed to gaze out past the fighting and through the darkness. His knees buckled, and he dropped to the ground. His rifle fell to the side.

Buckner remained in that odd position, as if kneeling in prayer, until two of his fellow soldiers bent to his side.

He looked at one of them with unseeing eyes and slumped against his companion, dead.

The half-dozen or so Texans closest now paused as one to stare at the lifeless body of their fearless leader. All around them, bullets whistled in the gathering blackness, the deafening sound making no impression on those who now watched almost reverently.

Henry and Antonio witnessed the terrible moment, and both felt lumps growing in their throats, a mixture of shock and terror. Safe behind the tall breastworks ladder for the moment, the boys looked at each other, trying to comprehend the tragic loss.

Henry turned to say something to his brother. Leander had disappeared! Where was he? The dark clouds of gunsmoke made his eyes water and seeing even more difficult.

Henry's eyes caught Leander as he ran right for the wall, where Buckner's body lay. Henry jumped to his feet and took two quick steps from behind the wooden ladder.

"Leander!" he cried. But his brother could not have heard him in the middle of the chaos of the battle raging all around them. Henry watched as his brother zigzagged through the fighting Texans, bullets from above spitting sand at his feet.

"Leander!" Henry called again, desperately. Leander, a step from the wall now, peered down at Buckner who lay still in the midst of the jostling bodies around him. Henry's brother bent over his friend, kneeling next to two other Texans as they attempted to drag the Indian fighter's body away from the fort.

"LEANDER!" Henry screamed as if his lungs would burst. Antonio grabbed Henry by the shoulder and joined his voice in the shout. Leander, hearing no other sounds for that instant, twisted his face away from Buckner's body and looked upward, into the night sky. A shot, somehow heard apart from all the other battle sounds, rang out. Leander came to his feet suddenly, as if some unseen rope had pulled him from the ground, posed for a moment almost on his toes, and fell back to the earth, his left arm sprawling across the body of the man he had called a hero. Sand sputtered up from where the stricken man's head hit the ground.

"LEANDER!"

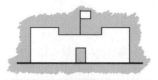

Chapter Seventeen

The fighting had stopped hours earlier. Now, just past midnight, Henry heard only an occasional shot fired into the blackness of the night. Threatening clouds covered the moon and stars.

Eight of John Austin's best sharpshooters remained on the battlefield, crouched behind pieces of driftwood dragged to spots less than a hundred yards from the fort. The other Texans had retreated to the safety of the dunes. They had carried the bodies of the dead and wounded off the beach. A physician bandaged gunshot wounds by dim candlelight.

On the parapets of the fort, Mexican soldiers stood watch. They fired no shots into the darkness now, having learned a terrible lesson that night. Whenever a Mexican shot into the dark, a bullet from a Texan's rifle returned with deadly accuracy, using the muzzle flash of the Mexican's escopeta as a target. A dozen times since the battle had stopped, a Mexican had fired and had fallen from the walkway, a bullet in his head.

For both sides, it now became a waiting game. At dawn, the attack would surely be renewed unless the colonel surrendered the fort.

In the Texan camp, men sat in small bunches around charcoal fires, well-hidden behind the sand dunes. The conversation continued but at a low pitch, and every once in awhile everyone stopped to listen to the groans of the wounded. A few men slept. Most talked through the night hours, reliving the battle, wondering aloud about what the dawn would bring.

The battle had ended poorly for the Texans. Someone had yelled a retreat, and half of the men had fallen back. No officer had given such a signal, however, and as they urged their forces forward, general confusion reigned on the battlefield. Men had run in all directions in the dark, bumping and falling, scattered by gunshots from the fort, unclear whose orders to obey.

The whole camp knew about Strap Buckner, how he had died at the walls of the fort, encouraging the Texans on to his last breath. The men who had marched from Fayette and Moore's Landing had dragged the bodies of two friends off the beach. Andy Castleman had been killed in the first charge, and his friend and neighbor, John Robinson, had been found dead as the men retreated to the dunes.

Three others had died of wounds they had received, but not everyone knew who had survived and who would be buried. Most thought that the next morning would bring more graves, perhaps, thought a few, their own.

Henry and Antonio sat together next to what had been a warming fire. Its last burning embers had just played out. They sat off to one side, away from most of the others. Neither spoke. They stared into the ground, listening to the distant rumble of thunder over the water.

Finally, after what seemed hours, Henry stood up and walked quietly across the camp, being careful not to step on anyone lying asleep. Men and gear lay scattered all over the dunes like the driftwood he had noticed before the sunset.

A fire brighter than the others spit flames and ashes into the sky, a soft black smoke rising to form its own low cloud above the dunes camp. Henry saw a man busily working over the prone body of one of the wounded Texans. The injured man jerked every now and then, his hands gripping a gun stock as the pain jolted through him.

"Doc," Henry called out quietly, "is he gonna be all right?"

The physician, a man from Brazoria, looked over at Henry's face, lit by the bonfire. He glanced back at his patient and then again to Henry. The doctor shook his head, shrugged his shoulders and went back to work. Battlefield hospitals were never very successful. And this young man had been seriously wounded. Henry knew the doctor could do little now, except try to make the man comfortable during the night.

"Henry!" a whispered voice stole through the darkness from behind. A man on a makeshift cot raised one arm in a wave toward him. "Henry! Come over here."

Henry turned and walked quickly to his brother's side. "Here I am, Leander. How're you doing?"

Leander winced as the pain below his left shoulder punched through him again. He had been unconscious for an hour after the battle ended. The boys had helped others carry him off, back to the dunes. The first thing Leander had said when he came to was, "What about Buckner?" They had told him the bad news straight out. No use lying about it. Leander had lay back and gritted his teeth with the news but had not said another word about it since. Now, he lay very still on the cot. As he gazed into his little brother's eyes, Leander tried to communicate what he felt inside, what he knew would happen soon. Henry felt a strange thump deep in his heart.

Henry made several more trips across the camp that evening to check on his big brother. Tonio accompanied him twice. Many of the Texans had made a point to speak to Leander, commending him on his bravery during the battle. Austin had come over, and Henry Smith and Wharton, too. Mr. Smith had even spoken to Henry, making sure the boy realized what a hero Leander was. That made Henry feel very proud!

The boys learned that Captain Russell had survived the battle as well. One of the crew members had been killed by a cannon shot, and the deck boasted two new holes in it. Before retiring up the river out of range for the night, Russell's cannon had done its own damage on the fort's entry gate. Henry hoped that Jeremiah was all right, but no one seemed to know around the camp.

"Leander, you better get some sleep," Henry said to his brother at his last visit that night, gripping his hand tightly. And, not knowing what else to say, he turned and walked toward the dark camp.

"See you in the morning, li'l brother," Leander called after him.

Henry and Antonio tried to stay awake, but it was no use. They had been up for twenty hours, had ridden miles, sailed as stowaways, walked from Munson's plantation, and fought in a battle with the Mexican army. That was plenty of adventure for one day. Around two o'clock that morning, both boys fell asleep. Nothing short of gunfire could have awakened them.

Except the rain. A huge thunderclap struck the camp just before first light, followed by a pelting rain that quickly became a downpour. The boys scrambled for any cover they could find, shuffling into a friend's tent but already drenched from the deluge. Rivulets of water eroded the dunes as water cascaded down onto the beach.

The hot summer shower seemed like it would never stop.

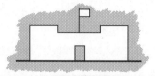

Chapter Eighteen

Two hours after daylight, a sopping wet Texas camp was roused from its covers by a single shot splitting the silence from somewhere within the camp. As the rain continued to flood the coastal plains, Antonio watched the men unwrap themselves from the dunes and stand at readiness. Rifles appeared from under blankets and saddlebags.

William Wharton sat on horseback waving his wide-brimmed hat in the air as his mount stepped lightly from puddle to puddle. Soon, a crowd gathered around him, forcing him to halt and make whatever announcement he had come to tell the men.

Antonio heard the shot, and shoved against the brown blanket next to him. Inside the blanket, trying in vain to keep dry, Henry Woods stirred himself awake. A shock of hair appeared from the blanket, then two eyes and a nose.

"What is it?" Henry asked sleepily.

"A signal, Henry. Wake up!" Tonio nudged his friend again, a little harder this time.

Henry threw off the wet blanket and grabbed his hat in the same motion. Following Antonio out of the tent, he peered through the morning rains. A crowd gathered around Mr. Wharton.

"Great news, men!" Wharton started. The two teen-agers pushed their way into the crowd. "Look to the fort!" he called out. As one, the men turned in the same direction.

Through the rain, as the sky brightened out over the water, a soldier from Point Bolivar spotted it first and called out.

"A flag!" he called. "A white flag flying above the walls!"

"Hurrah!" shouted the Texans. A white flag meant surrender. Ugartechea was giving up.

Smith and Austin joined Wharton a few minutes after the sighting and rode across the beach where they had fought the fierce battle. Ten others on horseback accompanied them, acting as bodyguards.

The boys stood as if they had been planted in the same spot, waiting for the men to return. Water ran off their hat brims in steady streams. Fifteen minutes passed, then another half-hour. Still no word, no sighting of the surrender party. Some of the men looked at each other with suspicion. Could it have been a trap, they wondered aloud?

One hour after the officers had left the camp, someone pointed into the gray mist. Ghostly shadows appeared on phantom horses. Wharton and the others had returned. The rain cloaked them until they emerged only fifty yards from the dunes.

As the platoon reached the edge of the camp, Henry could see a wide grin on the face of Mr. Smith. It had really happened: the battle at Velasco had come to an end.

Texans clapped each other on their backs, some giving out loud Whoops! and dancing in the soppy sand. Tonio and Henry turned to one another and shook hands. Tonio laughed out loud.

"C'mon, compadre," the Mexican boy said. "Let's go tell your brother." Henry ran, already a step ahead, dashing through the crowded camp.

They found Leander lying under a dark green blanket on the physician's cot. He tried to wave at the boys but grimaced in pain instead. Henry slid to a stop at Leander's side, already telling him the news.

"Surrendered!" he explained breathlessly. "Mr. Smith and Mr. Wharton just rode into camp. It's over! We've won!"

"That's great news, li'l brother," Leander whispered as he managed a weak smile.

"Tonio and I are going to the fort later today," Henry said, excited now at the thought. "Gosh, I wish you could come with us."

"No, thanks," Leander replied. He looked off in the general direction of the presidio for a moment. "I don't think I could ever go back to that place again."

The boys stood quietly. He was right, of course. At the base of that wall Captain Buckner had died and Leander himself had been shot. Only bad memories remained there. Henry regretted that he had mentioned it at all.

"But you two," Leander continued, noticing his brother's frown, "you need to go see it. We may never get back this way again. You go on now. Don't ever forget what happened here." He smiled at his brother one last time and closed his eyes.

For the first time in days, Henry just wanted to go home.

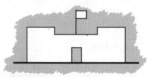

Chapter Nineteen

The boys never went back to the fort.

By mid-morning of that day, the twenty-seventh of June, the rain had quit. From a distance, Antonio and Henry watched the Mexican troops march out and form several lines in front of the gate. Above them the Texans busied themselves with the cannon perched on its parapet like a dangerous black bird. It would be hauled away from the beach, probably on to Bell's Landing.

In the afternoon, after Colonel Ugartechea's soldiers had been marched away toward Munson's plantation, a bugle call echoed its lonely song for funeral rites. It would have been impossible to carry the bodies of the seven slain Texans to their homes, so the decision was made to bury them near where they had fallen, fighting for Texas.

The men dug seven graves in the sand dunes and laid the wrapped bodies there.

Reverend Cloud led a brief service, concluding it with a prayer. The Texans straggled away in small groups, leaving behind only a few to finish the burial rites. Henry stayed at his brother's grave for a few extra moments. The memory of watching the battle at the fort seemed like a nightmare from a thousand years ago. He left the sight only after the men placed crosses made from driftwood at the head of each grave.

★ ★ ★

Antonio and Henry rode on the buckboard with the driver, a man named McNeill. He would take the boys as far as San Felipe, where others would see them on home to Woods' Prairie. While Henry kept his eyes on the road straight ahead, wiping away an occasional tear with his sleeve, Antonio stared back across the beach until the fort disappeared over the horizon. He turned around to watch the trail ahead, occasionally leaning forward as if to hurry the trip along.

★ ★ ★

The journey home took ten days. Bell's Landing brought the first real meal any of them had had in days, and a good night's sleep in the local inn. The boys retrieved their horses that had been left behind when they stowed away on the schooner. The next leg of the trip, to San Felipe, proved uneventful, although it rained off and on during those miles.

San Felipe de Austin stirred, alive with the news of the battle at Velasco, treating the boys as heroes when they rode into town. People crowded around the wagon even before it had stopped in front of the livery stable. Some asked questions. Others stood respectfully alongside the brave young men, shaking their hands or offering food and rest overnight.

★　★　★

On the fifth morning of their trip, Mr. Castleman, a neighbor of the Woods family who had lost his son Andrew in the battle, arrived in San Felipe and offered to take the boys home with him. Henry thought that Mr. Castleman acted very bravely, the way he had taken the news about his son. But the older man expressed his grief in his own silent way and spoke instead of the great sacrifice his son had made for the people of Texas.

"This is hard country, boys," Castleman said. "We all fight for our lives each day in different ways. But if something's worth fighting for, like Texas, we have to stand up when it's time and do what's right. I'm right proud of Andrew." He paused and looked straight at Henry. "As you should be of your brother." Henry jutted his jaw and squared his shoulders in response.

Castleman looked out over the crowd. "It's time to go home, men. Time to go home."

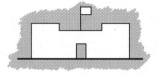

Epilogue

A month later, Henry sat on the top rail of the corral in front of Antonio's ranch house, looking over a letter he had written to Captain Russell. He had worked on it for some time and, although pleased with it, wanted his friend to approve.

"Listen to this, Tonio," Henry said. "Tell me what you think." The letter read:

August 1, 1832

Dear Captain Russell,

Thank you for your letter. It takes a long time for mail to get across the colony, but it sure was nice to hear from you, sir. Antonio and I are fine.

We returned home more than two weeks ago, safe and sound.

We told everyone around Woods' Prairie what happened on the Brazos. You were brave to sail right into battle!

I was glad to hear that Mr. Jeremiah is all right and was sorry for the man you lost. Next time you come west, I sure hope you will stop in for a visit. Pa says he'd like to shake the hand of any man who fights for Texas!

Your friend, Henry Woods

p.s. Thanks for watching over your stow-aways. We'll never forget our adventure!

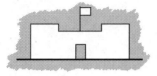

Author's Note

All of the characters in this story are real, except two. Antonio Gonzales and Crooked Path, though fictional, represent the young boys who lived on the Texas frontier in those adventurous, exciting days.

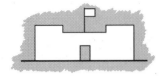

About the Author

Paul N. Spellman is a Texas storyteller who teaches history at Houston Community College, University of Houston and Duchesne Academy in Houston.

He is finishing his doctoral dissertation—a biography of early Texas leader Colonel Hugh McLeod—at University of Houston. Mr. Spellman earned a master's degree in Texas history from the University of Texas at Austin and a bachelor's degree in English from Southwestern University in Georgetown, Texas.

Mr. Spellman has researched the pioneer Woods family extensively, providing background for his realistic characterizations of Zadock, Minerva, Leander and Henry Woods and others. He has written two other historical adventures featuring *Race to Velasco* characters Henry Woods, Antonio Gonzales and Crooked Path, which are yet to be published.

His next project involves a story of a sister and brother after the 1900 Galveston flood.

Suggested Reading

Students

Davis, Joe Tom. *Legendary Texians, Volume III*. Austin, Texas: Eakin Press, 1986.

_____. *Legendary Texians, Volume IV*. Austin, Texas: Eakin Press, 1989.

Hoff, Carol. *Wilderness Pioneer: Stephen F. Austin of Texas.* Dallas: Hendrick-Long Publishing Co., 1987.

Sorenson, Richard. *Indian Tribes of Texas: The Customs, Beliefs, and Traditions of the Texas Indian Cultures.* Portland, Texas: Teacher Enrichment, 1994.

Teachers

Barker, Eugene C. *The Life of Stephen F. Austin: Founder of Texas, 1793–1836.* Austin: Texas State Historical Association, 1949.

Duval, John. *Early Times in Texas.* Austin: H.P.N. Gammel & Co., Publishers, 1892.

Fehrenbach, T. R. *Lone Star: A History of Texas and the Texans.* New York: Macmillan, 1968.

Gray, Robert, ed. *A Visit to Texas in 1831.* Houston: Cordovan Press, 1975.

Hatcher, Mattie Austin. *Letters of an Early American Traveller: Mary Austin Holley, Her Life and Her Works, 1784–1846.* Dallas: Southwest Press, 1933.

Smithwick, Noah. *The Evolution of a State.* Austin: Gammel Book Company, 1900.

Vigness, David M. *The Revolutionary Decades: Texas, 1810–36.* Austin: Steck-Vaughn, 1965.

Also,

Spellman, Paul N. *Zadock and Minerva Cottle Woods, American Pioneers.* (Unpublished but available from the author.)